Dreams in Incarceration

Inspired by Real-Life Events

Cillian Dunne

Copyright © Cillian Dunne

Introduction

What you are about to read is a hyper-visualization of the reality that most inmates face in California prisons. While the characters portrayed in this book deserved to be incarcerated for a variety of reasons, my goal was to humanize them and give them three-dimensional representation. Regardless of their past, many of them are still individuals who lie awake at night, haunted by the horrifying crimes they have committed. It is true that there are many prisoners out there that lack the desire to improve and will remain incarcerated until their last breath, but there are also plenty of individuals like Dave who fight every single day to become better. It was Dave's unwavering dedication to a transformed life that captivated me and led me to share his incredible and harrowing story. Dave hopes that his story can not only inspire people in prison to turn their lives around, but he also hopes that young children who may follow in his footsteps see it as a cautionary tale.

With all that being said...

This book blends the harsh reality of the physical struggles that inmates face with the surreal psychological night terrors that consume the minds of criminals as they fester in their cells.

Enjoy.

Table of Contents

Introduction 1

The Defense Rests 4

Two Shots, One Cell 13

Mom's First Visitation 20

A Nightmare in Incarceration 25

Everyone's an Expert 29

Incubus 44

Getting Out of the Hole 50

Days of Movement 61

The Gym 66

Caged Animals 76

The First Domino 80

Back in Business 92

A Proustian Premonition 103

The Final Domino 109

Room Number 15 125

Predators & Prey 130

The First Date 142

Trouble in Block One 149

A Nightmare in Inglewood 159

Going All In 166

The King of the Jungle 178

A Dream in Incarceration 190

I am David Spivey 194

The Defense Rests

Before I was a criminal, I was a kid. I had friends in the neighborhood, a little brother, a mother, and a big family stretching from Los Angeles to Mississippi. I could go outside whenever I wanted and play with whoever I wanted. I had dreams for my future that only I could see. I was smart and everyone knew that I was capable of something, especially my mother. She prioritized my education and gave me constant encouragement to do something more with my life.

I loved to talk. My trap would run twenty-four hours a day. I bet my mama wished she had bought some earplugs the way my brother and I would bicker and yell in our family home in South Central. Still, she gave us the love we needed as children. She never stopped giving that affection, even as my life progressed into the hood. My mother knew my path, and she tried everything to stop me from falling into that hole, but there was nothing she could do, even when I was little. I had already slapped the cuffs on and tied myself to the radiator. She knew that one day the heat would either kill me or make me appreciate the cold.

When you're seven years old growing up in the neighborhood, you have a lot of friends. Everybody's got kids running around. I had a whole group of guys and girls on my block, and whenever we were bored, we would go over to Auntie Cheryl's house. South Central is a big place with a lot of people, but everyone knew that woman. She was a mama goose to a lot of kids. We would all play together and she fed us and made sure we were getting enough water. It was better than being out on the street where trouble lingered. Some other kids I knew were getting into grown-up shit before they even turned ten. This made me jealous at the time. All my friends and I thought being in a gang was cool, even if we didn't fully understand what it meant to be associated with that world. I knew that there were some kids out there who were in the backseat of their older brother's car, laying back and gazing up at the baby blue California sky, shielding their eyes from the glowing sun that laid rays of light down onto the sizzling Angelino streets below. Meanwhile, me and the rest of them were at Auntie Cheryl's.

Auntie Cheryl would make sure her rules were enforced when the kids all played on her property. Firstly, she did not tolerate violence of any kind. She believed in being civil and talking problems out. Secondly, she did not allow the use of curse words. If a "fuck" or a "shit" slipped out, she'd have your ass beet red with a wooden spoon grasped tightly in her hand. Lastly, if for whatever reason one of these things did occur and there was a doubt of guilt, all children would be required to stop playing and gather for a trial to decide whether or not the rule-breaker was to be reprimanded. Auntie Cheryl was not only the sheriff, but she was the judge and the jury. These kids who already had a taste of the gang life would have never survived under her jurisdiction.

Before I wanted to be a gangster, I wanted to be just like Johnnie Cochran. My little, awe-inspired eyes would watch him on TV and witness historical cases being won and lost at the mercy of my idol.

Everybody talks about his involvement in the OJ case, but I thought that everything he did was golden. He possessed the devil's tongue but used it to free brothers and sisters, whether they were guilty or not. I respected him, and a seven-year-old boy in South Central doesn't usually have respect for anyone that isn't their blood. He was a professional wizard of his craft, casting spells of disenchantment over courtrooms and intoxicating them with his words of persuasion. I knew deep down I was capable of the same kind of influence. I was a motherfuckin' talented kid who always knew how to get out of a pinch. So, when Lil' Mike called Markus a "motherfuckin' cocksucker" one day during a game of tag, Auntie Cheryl came running outside, grabbed Markus by the scruff of his neck, and accused him of using the language. "It was Lil' Mike," Markus yelled. Auntie Cheryl did not believe him. She was an old woman but a sharp woman, and she wasn't letting go of the fact that the devil's language echoed through her home. I knew that it was my time to put my skills to use and defend my brother.

"My client is innocent," I yelled to Auntie Cheryl from across the yard.

"I heard him with my own two ears, and I ain't deaf, young man," Auntie Cheryl responded.

"I want a trial," I said to her, standing up straight with my hands on my hips.

"Everybody go into the living room," she said to us all.

Markus was sitting on a wooden dinner chair before the group of us. There must have been a dozen kids all sitting on the carpet, gazing up at Markus as his legs dangled above the floor. Everybody was getting rowdy when Lil' Mike stood up and asked "Where is Auntie

Cheryl?" The kids were starting to grow impatient with excitement. This was our trial of the century. Everybody knew that Markus was innocent. Lil' Mike was taunting him with a cheeky smile plastered onto his face, but when Auntie Cheryl walked into that room with a white Thomas Jefferson wig on her head, she dragged a chair up next to Markus. The screeching of the wood echoed through the room. Everyone shut up and paid attention, especially Lil' Mike.

"We're here today for the trial of Markus Washington, who is being accused of using the devil's language... How do you plead?"

"Not guilty, your honor," Markus said with a shake in his high-pitched voice.

"And who will be representing you today?"

"I will, your honor," I said as I stood up and put my hands behind my back.

The kids cheered and yelled like a group of soccer hooligans after their team scored a goal. Auntie Cheryl raised her index finger and zipped them all up. The tension lingered in the air as I stood before her, my client shaking in his boots as his future flashed before his eyes. "Mr. Spivey, are you aware that if I find your client guilty, then not only will he get a spankin', but he also will not be allowed to play video games for one week?" The room went silent. All eyes moved toward me as my brain processed the severity of this punishment. No video games for a week, man, that would have killed Markus. He was the best of us. Mortal Kombat, Mario... It didn't matter, he would win because he would play the most.

"I am aware of the repercussions, ma'am," I said confidently.

"Okay, plead his case," she said as she leaned back in her chair and crossed her arms.

Markus was a sweet kid, but he had a loud mouth, too. He and Lil' Mike were like brothers. They were so close that it was even hard to distinguish who was who when you were looking at them. So, I knew my case had to be better than just getting both of them to repeat what was said so that Auntie Cheryl could hear the difference between the two voices. I also understood that Auntie Cheryl, in this case, was the victim. It was she who pressed these charges against Markus. Being innocent until proven guilty is a farce, especially when you've got so many people with their eyes on you. Nobody pays attention to an innocent man, only a guilty man who claims he is innocent.

"Your honor, how long have you known my client?"

"Since he was four years old," she responded.

"And in the five years that you have known him, how many times has he been on trial?"

"He ain't never been on trial," she said.

The room gasped as if I had just cracked the case. Lil' Mike gulped as the boys and girls around him laughed and taunted him with gentle nudges and pushes. Auntie Cheryl raised her index finger and the room fell silent. She then slowly turned her head to face me. Our eyes locked, she remained relaxed in her seat with her arms crossed. "And?" she said with a shrug of her shoulders.

"And, in those five years, how many times has Lil' Mike been on trial?"

"Too many," she said as she looked right into Lil' Mike's eyes.

The children laughed. Everybody knew that Lil' Mike was trouble. He was a cute kid, all the mothers thought so. Mike could get out of a jam with one pout. This was not one of those times. Back then, I thought I had to give Auntie Cheryl a trail of breadcrumbs. She would eat information one piece at a time, like a trail of breadcrumbs. I thought it was genius. In a way, I guess it was.

"I call Lil' Mike to the stand," I said as I turned to Lil' Mike and pointed at him.

The crowd erupted. All of the children started slamming their hands against the carpet floor as if it were a drum and they were marching to war. Lil' Mike gulped and hung his head low as he switched seats with Markus, who took his place on the floor amongst all of the other children. I removed my hands from behind my back and rubbed them together before Lil' Mike as the crowd's cheers slowly dimmed to silence. I cleared my throat and collected my thoughts. I had seen what had happened with my own eyes, but that wasn't a card I could play given the fact that I am Markus' lawyer. Auntie Cheryl needed proof or a confession, and I didn't have proof.

"Lil' Mike, how are you today?" I asked.

"Bad. This is a waste of time," he responded as he crossed his arms.

"Why is this a waste of time?"

"I want to play video games before I gotta go home. I don't got video games at home."

Auntie Cheryl cleared her throat and pointed to the old watch on her wrinkled wrist. I nodded to her, understanding that she didn't have all day. As soon as the sun would go down, we'd all have to go home. None of us knew what Auntie Cheryl did when night called. We didn't ever talk about it. All we knew was that the very next day we would be in her house playing and laughing with each other, just like we had done every single day beforehand. I didn't have long to prove that Markus was innocent. The ember glow of the falling sun illuminated

Auntie Cheryl's living room in a fiery golden light that dimmed as the seconds passed.

"Lil' Mike, can you tell me what Markus said?"

"No, I cannot," Lil' Mike responded.

"But, we were all playing tag, and you were it, weren't you?"

"I wasn't it," Lil' Mike exclaimed as he unfolded his arms.

"I think you were," I said with a smirk.

"I wasn't it, Markus was it," Lil' Mike said as he pointed at Markus.

"How did you know he was it?"

"Pfft. Everybody knows who's it," Lil' Mike said as he folded his arms together and shook his head.

I placed my hands behind my back and slowly paced side-to-side before the stand. Lil' Mike's eyes moved back and forth along with my movements like he was watching a match of tennis. Auntie Cheryl sat back in her judge's chair with a smirk. She could see that my trail of breadcrumbs had led her closer to the truth. I had to strike while the iron was hot. I needed Auntie Cheryl to be blinded by the intense steam that would rise from the lawful branding I wanted to imprint on Lil' Mike's forehead for all of us children to see, like a cow who had run off from the group and gotten caught at the electric fence.

"My client tagged you, didn't he?"

"No," Lil' Mike exclaimed.

"My client tagged you and you called him a motherfuckin' cocksucker in front of all of us, didn't you?"

"I didn't do shit!"

The room gasped. Every pair of little eyes gradually moved to face Auntie Cheryl, who shook her head at Lil' Mike. "You in trouble now, Lil' Mike," she said. I had done it. I had led Auntie Cheryl to the truth, and the truth was that a guilty man would continue to be guilty so long as he denies his guilt. All I had to do was entice him to prove it to us once again. Lil' Mike had the pottiest mouth of all potty mouths, but Markus did not. That's why they were such good friends, I think. They balanced each other out socially. When one was annoying you, you could always talk to the other one. I always understood people. It was my strength. I knew what someone wanted, I knew why they wanted it, and I knew what they would do to get it.

"Markus, you are an innocent man... Lil' Mike, no video games for one week, and I'm tellin' your mama'," Auntie Cheryl said.

"My momma ain't been home in a week, so good luck," Lil' Mike responded.

"Then, Imma' tell your daddy," Auntie Cheryl exclaimed with a shake of her head.

"No, no! Not my daddy, please," Lil' Mike fell at the feet of Auntie Cheryl.

Us kids all just laughed at him. He was begging for his life like we were being sent to the electric chair. No video games for a week was rough, and I didn't feel good about putting my brother away like that. If I had done that on the street, I'd be an outcast. I'd have never gotten to where I did and earned the respect that only a true brother could, and I was a true motherfuckin' brother. Still, I'll never forget what Auntie Cheryl said to me as I left her home that day. All the other kids were skipping out onto the front lawn, flaying their arms about with animated laughter and childhood debauchery.

"Can I talk to you for a second, Dave?" Auntie Cheryl said to me.

She hunkered down to my level and looked at me with her maple-brown eyes. "You a smart kid. Your mom thinks so, too. Everyone does," she said to me. "Thank you," I responded. I could hear the yells and cheers of my friends on the street. That's all I cared about. It was summertime and the smell of fresh grass lingered in the air. Though the sun was setting, it was still warm. I remember that warmth. I've been hot since, and I've been cold since, but I've never been that warm.

"A lot of kids you know are startin' to join gangs, ain't they?" she said to me.

"I don't know," I responded.

"Sure, you don't... Just remember what I say today, David. You can do more than that," Auntie Cheryl said gently as she placed her hand on my shoulder.

Auntie Cheryl removed her grasp from my shoulder and it felt like I was a balloon that lifted into the sky with no way back down to earth. I didn't have any control over where I wanted to go or what I wanted to do. The wind would carry me and gravity would push me in directions with destinations I knew nothing of. The ground was growing further away and my vision was thinning as the atmosphere grew more tense. The darkness of space was within sight, and I kept moving toward it. I don't even know if there was a way I could have been pinned down at that moment in time, and I didn't yet realize that the further I rose away from reality on earth, the closer I would get to popping.

Two Shots, One Cell

Two shots and it was all over. I was seventeen years old, and I was filled with angst. I had already been to juvie by then. I joined the gang early in my teen years and I did some bad shit. I didn't care about having a police record. I was a fighter, and I fought whoever was in my way. Juvie was a hot-tempered place. In a lot of ways, it's more violent than prison. If someone looked at you the wrong way in juvie, you had two choices. You could fight that motherfucker... You might win, or you might lose. The second choice was backing down. Whoever chose the second option didn't last long. It was kill or be killed, and I knew that I was a killer. What I did on the street had no true repercussions, because I knew that all that would happen was that I would get sent back to a cell and I'd have to fight for myself, just like I had always done.

Two shots, man. I can still hear them. I can visualize the bullets whizzing through the night air and the sound they made slicing through the victims' bodies as they ran from us through the neighborhood. That shot must have rung for miles. People in Santa Monica probably heard it. I remember how the car we were driving sounded, how it revved so loudly that we were a moving target for the police. As the bodies hit the floor, the tires screeched and steam exerted out of the exhaust pipe and covered the rear of our car with a smokey screen before we accelerated into the distance. The screams and yells of our victims echoed through the streets of Inglewood and seemed to linger in the air for minutes, no matter how fast we were driving, and how far away we were. I was instantly forced to marinate in the murder. That feeling ruptured me, and as we were driving, and we saw the flashing lights of the police behind us, we knew we were all going away for a long time.

The fastest getaway driver in Los Angeles couldn't have gotten out of this pinch. The cops who pinned us to the gravel of the street below smelled of cigarettes and coffee. The policeman who had his knee on my back was a fat guy with a beard. His partner stood idly by on his walkie, calling for backup. "We got some Crips down here," he spoke into the device. I could just close my eyes and shake my head. They could tell we were gangsters from a mile away. Anyone could. It was important to us and to the higher-ranking members that we honor the gang and wear our colors with pride. We were just kids trapping at the lowest tier in a society of criminals. We thought we were gangsters, but we were just kids... Kids who saw two rival gang members in their neighborhood and conspired to murder them. Kids who stalked and hunted these victims like prey, as if we were lions hunting gazelles. I'll never forget that night and how I felt. I had always called myself a killer in juvie, but now I was, and I found myself as a seventeen-year-old man going to a state prison.

One died, one lived. Murder and conspiracy to murder. This got me life. "The People vs. David Spivey"... the headline may as well have been flashing in lights in Times Square. Everyone heard about it. They all knew what I did and that there was no way we were innocent. 100 years to life. Thank God it was commuted down to 15 to life by Governor Brown. I bet some people from the neighborhood were happy that I was going away. I was an aggressor and some folk held a lot of hate in their heart for me. If it weren't for my mama, I think just about everyone in the neighborhood would have lost all hope for me. They knew what kind of mother she was, and they knew that me being in this cell had nothing to do with the way she raised me. Me being here was my doing and my doing alone.

My first cellie was a brother named Star. That wasn't his real name, but that's what he demanded to be called. He was skinny and tall, like a basketball player. I didn't necessarily trust Star. We grew up in different neighborhoods of Los Angeles. He was in a gang, too. He rolled with guys that were neither an allie nor an enemy. We would rarely speak, out of loyalty for our own gangs. I had never heard of him before prison, but we knew some of the same people. It was both of our first time in prison. He was inside for grand theft auto and attempted murder. He looked at a man the wrong way in a crowded Long Beach bar and a fight broke out. Star was a big dude, and he beat that guy easily. He beat him so much that the brother almost died. Star tried getting out of there as quickly as possible, so he took the dude's car keys from his back jeans pocket. Star couldn't drive in a straight line to save his life. He got caught and there we were. I didn't learn any of this from the horse's mouth, I learned through whispers in the yard.

The yard is where everyone would congregate. We were in A yard. We were among the GP. That's General Population. Outside of that, you had PC, or Protective Custody. Depending on the size of the prison, there could have been more, or even less isolation. I can only speak to what I saw. On the perimeter of A yard, you'd have guards patrolling the fence and standing in overlook towers. Even if they weren't there, I doubt anyone could have escaped. The fence rose dozens of feet into the air, and on top was some barbed wire. If you had tried to scale that wall, you'd either tear your flesh up, or you'd make it over and fall to your death on the other side. What was contained by the four walls of the fence were some of the most dangerous people in the state of California. I was one of them, and people knew it right when I showed up on my first day in the yard. The beating California sun sent rays of fire down onto the dusty courtyard below.

"Yo Dave!"

A familiar raspy voice called from a group of men sitting on some rafters. I recognized a few. The man who yelled my name was Philly. I called him that because I'm an Eagles fan, and so was he. We both joined the gang around the same time, but people trusted me more because he had a couple of DP's as a teenager. A DP was like having a record in the gang. It meant you disobeyed orders and were reprimanded for them. That shit doesn't wash away. It stays with you every day you're in the gang. Older members recognize who you are, not by your name, but by your record. Philly wasn't as trusted as I was out there, but in here it looked like he was. He was rolling with a crew of us, all cut from the same cloth. It was without question that these men would be my friends until the day I died, or until I decided to transfer institutions.

In prison, there were a lot of people you didn't associate with in the yard. White folk were also off-limits. Those skinheads were just as nasty as we were. It was like signing your death note if you went up and spoke to one of them in the yard. There were some exceptions inside the jailhouse, but not in the yard. Then, you had the Mexicans and their multitude of gangs like the Norteños and the Sureños. We didn't always see eye-to-eye with the Hispanics, but there was a certain level of respect. They always rode in big groups like us. The Asians were influential. There were so many of them, man. Almost all of them rode in crews from East LA. They were dangerous motherfuckers, too. They had a dude named Xing who rocked with their group who could make mini-swords. The rest of us knew how to sharpen a piece of metal, but Xing knew how to make fucking artillery. If you messed with an Asian dude, you were getting shanked.

When I looked around the yard, it was these racially segregated groups that dominated the population, but there were outliers. There were always independent guys who felt morally disgusted by associating with a gang. To do that you needed to have balls, because if something happened to you, nobody had your back. Then, you had some smaller racial groups such as the Islanders or Native Americans. The indigenous guys were popular because they had money. I learned that all of these Native guys were being sent cash from their tribe every 30 days. Four thousand dollars a month, on average. They were able to buy anything they wanted, and one thing about prison is, there are a whole lot of people trying to sell something. I looked around that yard and saw just about every category of man you could find until I saw that decrepit fucking slithering scumbag.

"Is that Puma?" I asked Philly.

"You know that motherfucker?"

"Yeah, we were in the same juvie for a few months," I said as I stared Puma down from across the yard.

Puma was a big motherfucker. He weighed two hundred and seventy pounds, easy. He had a short afro and always cut the sleeves off his clothes. He did that in juvie, and he did that in prison, too. My heart beat fast when I saw him in the yard. My fist tightened and my vision centered on that beastly asshole. He would constantly lick his thick, chapped lips with his slightly blue tongue. His eyebrows were as bushy as his afro and they moved with every exaggerated movement of his face. He would touch other kids in prison, and when they fought back, he'd fight harder. He was a freak. A rapist. A motherfucker who I was not going to look at every day and ask myself when he was going to make a move. Everybody on the outside seems to think that prison rape is a commonality. It's not. If somebody raped another dude, you bet your ass that the rapist would get shanked within 24 hours. Every prison I've ever been in has been like this. Puma was the only guy I knew doing it, and the only reason he got away with it for so long was because he was crazier than any motherfucker who would try to stop him. He was unshankable. He was a lurking creature that stalked his prey on the tips of his toes. I couldn't imagine a prison where a man like him could run rampant.

    I paced toward Puma as he smoked a cigarette by himself. His frame was the largest in the yard by a country mile. He towered over other inmates and cast shadows onto them. He was gazing over at a group of white men lifting weights. He even licked his lips a couple of times. I was angry. I was rageful, and on my first day of a life sentence, I wanted to kill him.

    "Puma, you remember me?" I yelled as I charged toward him.

    "Nah," he responded as he licked his lips, holding the cigarette down by his side.

    "We were in juvie together," I said as I got close to him and squared up. I could see dudes from all segregated groups turning and gazing over at us. I even saw some bloods discontinuing their conversation so they could have eyes on me. If I strayed too far away from my pack, they could eat me alive. "Come here, Puma," I said as I gestured for him to lean in toward me. A smile struck Puma's face and his eyes widened. His gaze started at my toes and slowly worked its way up my body, over my groin and stomach, and gradually up to my face. He stared into my soul. I stared back. "I remember you, Spivey," he said with a chuckle.

I grabbed Puma by the collar and dragged him close. The hot air from my nostrils and mouth hit him in the face. He had the skin of a man who had spent every waking moment of his life in the sun. "If you lay a goddamn finger on me, I'll stab you in the fucking throat," I whispered to him. Puma puckered his lips together and blew a fake kiss. I let go of that motherfucker and pushed him a few steps back. He stood there, chuckling. He was vile. I turned and walked through hordes of dudes to get back to my own. Everyone was looking at me. I was being scanned especially by the gangs who were my sworn enemies. A motherfucker that I would come to know as Chains eyed me up real good.

Everyone knew who Puma was, that's why he didn't have anyone. He wasn't even independent, he was just a freak. His stench lingered long after I left. I still had some on my hands, and it took days to go away. Two shots, man. All it took was two shots for me to end up in that place. I was a thug. I was still the same guy I was on the street. I did not give a fuck, and it would have been the death of me. If it weren't for my mother, I'd still be shaving a shank, ready to poke Puma in the stomach at the first sight of malicious intent.

Mom's First Visitation

It wasn't long before my mom came to visit me in prison. A lot of guys in incarceration had loved ones who came to them regularly. Puma didn't, but just about everyone else did. Star's brother and his wife would visit him once a week and they'd catch up. The inmates that couldn't hack the loneliness would see the prison therapist. It took a lot of self-convincing to see that figure in incarceration. A lot of dudes saw the therapist to try and get drugs prescribed, especially the more opportunistic thinkers. Only some of the patients were genuine. I was dreading that first visit. I had a certain dichotomy where one half of me didn't give a fuck what anyone thought, and the other half would just want to talk to his mom. I never said that shit out loud in prison, but you could tell dudes felt the same way. I sat in my cell, lying on my bed and gazing up at the gray ceiling, waiting for a guard to come and escort me down to the visitation hall.

Minutes in my cell would pass slowly in the beginning. I had a few amenities to keep me entertained, like an old radio. Star had a TV with the speakers taken out. The guards were cool with these devices, as long as you obeyed their rules. The television had to be silent. The guards didn't want every cell on the block blasting entertainment at full volume. They did however allow us to have a radio. As long as you kept it down to a reasonable volume, they would let you keep it and use it. The day my mama was visiting, I didn't care about that stuff. I wanted the minutes to pass slowly. I didn't want to be entertained. I wanted to feel the purgatory of that place. Star was lying on his bed doing the same thing. The only sounds that filled the air were the clanking of booted shoes against the metal staircases and hallways that circumnavigated the block I was confined in.

"Yo Dave," I heard from across the cell.

"What's up, Star?"

"You want a Xanax?"

"Sure."

I took the pill and swallowed it. I knew that it would put me in a place where I didn't have to think about what my mama was going to be telling me. I could just sit back and relax and not be reminded about being in that prison. That was wishful thinking. I did some hard drugs in my life and none of them made me forget that I was a cold-blooded gangster. That was in my bones. It was imprinted onto my soul. I was a killer and a menace to society. A Xanax could only do so much.

"Your ma' is visiting today?" Star asked.

"Yeah," I responded as I continued to gaze up at the ceiling with my hands behind my head.

Boots clanked outside the cell and grew louder with each passing second. "Spivey," a yell came from outside my cage. It was a guard ready to escort me to the visitation room. He stood upright and had his hands on his hips. "I'm comin'," I told him. I sauntered alongside the guard as we passed by cell after cell. From the outside, it looked like a zoo. The newer inmates would sometimes rush to the bars and reach out. The seasoned guys would stay in bed, doing whatever they were doing, but they'd watch you.

Somebody always had their eye on you in prison. The guard stopped before a bolted door. He removed a key card and scanned it. As it opened, a flood of chatter, laughter, and crying filled the air. I stepped inside and was met by the open-floor visitation room. The walls were bland and colorless. Two dozen white tables filled the space, with three backless chairs at each one. It was like a high school cafeteria. I scanned the room. I saw a sea of orange overalls sitting opposite streetwear. I moved my gaze from left to right until I saw her.

My mother's name was Linda. She was beautiful, and on this day, she wore black. I sauntered toward her as if I had rocks in my shoes. She rose and opened her arms to me and when I fell into them I felt a rush of pain flow through my veins and shoot into my heart. If it weren't for the Xanax, I would've trembled. "Sit down, ma," I said to her as I released myself. We sat opposite each other in silence at first. The chatter around us was loud. I didn't know what to say, she didn't either. When I was in juvie, she would always come in guns blazing. She had news and would keep me up-to-date on what everyone in the family and the neighborhood was up to. Not that time. That time, she was speechless.

"It's good to see you, ma," I said to her.

"How have you been holding up?" She asked.

"You know me, ma. I'll be fine no matter where I'm at."

She gazed down to her neatly dressed shoes and took a deep breath. She couldn't even look me in the eyes. "Ma," I said as I leaned over the table and reached out to her. She just shook her head and kept her arms by her side. "Ma," I repeated. She leaned back in her chair and crossed her arms. "It's your fault you're in here, David," she said to me. I sat back in my chair and pulled my arms across the table. I couldn't believe she would say that to me. I was her son and I knew she loved me. She was one of the only people who truly did at the time. I was seventeen years old, and as rebellious as a late-teen could be, but he would still need affirmation from his mother. I was blind at that moment.

"William joined a gang," she muttered to me as she put her head in her hands.

William was my younger brother. He was a good kid and my mom didn't want him following my path. He was smart, too, but I knew he would swim in my wake. In our neighborhood, it was one of the only options for him to do something with his life. He followed rules and people liked him, especially older dudes who had been rising up the ranks themselves. William was funny, and he always made my mom laugh. "It's your fault, David," she followed. The room that was once filled with chatter, laughter, and tears was now silent. All that remained was me and my mom. I couldn't even see anyone else. It was all a blur... Everything but her.

"I'm still gonna' visit you, baby, and you know I love you... But you need to accept that this is the life you've chosen for not only yourself but for your brother and me, too."

"I'm sorry," I responded.

"Not today you're not, but someday you will be," she said lowly.

The visitation room boiled to a thousand degrees and my vision wavered. The blurred figures of inmates and their loved ones swam through the air as if I were looking through a hazy pane of glass. My heart beat fast and my face trembled as I tried to process the complexity of my emotions. I couldn't let anyone in the room see me break down, and I couldn't wait until I got back to my cell because I didn't trust Star yet. All I could do was swallow my feelings and puff my chest out. I was a tough motherfucker and I wouldn't let that image sway, not even for my mother.

A Nightmare in Incarceration

We are hunters who load up our rifles and creep through the grass. The wind sways and sings a song of death as my brothers and I tip-toe along the outer banks of our prey's watering hole. We can see a whole group of them congregating outside. They're the same ones who taunted us. They are our sworn enemies and our tribe leaders demand we hunt them and kill them as a show of pride and power in the concrete jungle.

The street is full of us, youthful and elderly. Older guys in the gang pull up, smoke a blunt, and then head out to do whatever they want. They bark orders at us. They berate us. Younger guys stay together. We take the orders we're given. Today and every day, we are told to show strength. We are prideful creatures who will do anything to retain our status as badass motherfuckers. We stand on that stoop with our heads held high and on a swivel.

A group of women pass by on the street and I call them over. "Hey, where you going?" I start talking to a chick named Lashandra while my boys take care of her friends. She's wearing red leather, and she looks good. Me and Lashandra have chemistry. We're young and full of hormones and all we want to do is jump into bed. It couldn't be more obvious by the way she looks up at me with her big, round eyes. She flutters her lashes slowly as I tell her about my shoe collection at home. "Lashandra," a female voice echoes. One of her friends has somewhere to be, so Lashandra gives me her number and tells us to roll over to her girl's party later that night. "I better see you, Spivey," she whispers to me while grabbing my forearm.

"Yo guys, look over there," a deep voice bellows.

We turn our heads slowly like a pack of lions watching a herd of gazelle run by them. Before us are two guys in a beat-up Chevy. They roll by us slow enough that we can see their faces, but fast enough so that we can't do anything about it. "Those motherfuckers are in our neighborhood," someone yells from the group. Every lion in the pack stands on all four legs and perches upright as they watch the gazelles run off into the distance. We're disrespected. Prey should never flaunt themselves through a lion's territory. If I wandered into their neighborhood, they'd be the killers. They'd run after me with their claws out and mouths salivating with rage. We're not going to act any differently.

"We can't allow that shit," another voice echoes.

The pack grows restless as murderous statements and vicious hypotheticals bounce from mouth to mouth. They want these boys dead, and so do I. I'm willing to do anything for the blue. I cock my gun and nod to a couple of the guys. They remove their weapons and check the bullets in the chambers. We're ready for the hunt. The car revs and smoke and dust kick up behind us as we speed off down the street. I'm sitting in the back, looking out the window as we leave our neighborhood. The familiar homes and storefronts blur as we whizz by. "Keep your eyes open," I say. The territory we're driving into is dangerous. I'd rather be in the Amazon rainforest with a machete and anti-venom than be here with a loaded gun and a tank full of gas. We can't roll our windows down because if we do, then some fools from this neighborhood will hunt us just like we are hunting their brothers.

We lick our lips as our eyes scan every car and home. We know there are a couple of places they could be. We hear about them through whispers on the street. Across the great plains of South Central, word travels fast and into your enemies' ears without warning. In this part of town, the gang lords have their watering holes and hang-out spots, just like we do. All of the creatures will congregate and drink from the same pool of water. Day or night, they'll roll in crews and be ready to fight at any moment. The fact that we are all the same is never lost on me, but someone must prevail as king of the jungle.

We're quiet as we move through the streets. The sound of the purring engine and jingling keys fill the air. The moon is bright and high in the sky. The stars are barely visible behind a thin layer of smog that hangs gently in the atmosphere. A wave of shivers run up my spine. My eyes grow wide, and my hand slowly grasps tightly around the butt of my gun. In the near distance, I can see the car they were driving. There are silhouettes near it. They're all standing outside of the Hollywood Park Motel as a layer of fog gradually sinks to the earth from the dark sky above.

We hunch our backs as we peer through the grass and watch our unknowing prey. Our growls rumble in the silent air and our breathing is slow and steady. I can feel the power running through me as I lock eyes on my targets. We get as close as we can to them. Our teeth are sharp. The moonlight illuminates their faces for just one moment before they catch a glimpse of us, but by then, it's too late. I unleash my force upon them and leave them crawling in a pool of their own life, dragging themselves back to their gang as our pride of lions flees the territory with blood dripping from our claws.

The shadows of the foggy streets surround us and strip us of our sight. We're propelling through the plains without any inkling as to what is following us or what is ahead. The screams of our prey echo through the misty air and the moonlight above is blocked and only grayness remains. The wind blows onto my face at the speed of light and I can feel my skin peeling back as the force ruptures my very soul. The screams never falter no matter how fast we drive. I feel the acid within my stomach bubble. My eyes grow wide with sharp pain and my brain beats like a drum. Red and blue flashing lights shimmer in the distance. It's no mirage. It's the only way forward, and it's the only sign of life in the future before me. I am going to die in prison.

Everyone's an Expert

I was waking up every night in a cold sweat. A series of nightmares were running through my brain. My heart pounded while I slept. I knew that it would come to be unbearable the longer I spent between those fucking four walls. When you pull gold out of the ground, it doesn't come out looking like a fine watch or a ring. It has impurities that need to be taken out. That's what incarceration felt like for me. My family and friends were the only people who knew I was a good person. I just needed to get the impurities out of me. But, I also had a name to uphold. I had a physique to mold and shape into a killing machine. If I got caught lacking in the yard, it could have been the end for me. Workouts were common and bulking was necessary. It wasn't like out on the street where dudes would be able to hit a gym and then a food joint afterward. We had a schedule and it was a dogfight to get to those weights. I worked on my physicality like a bull, but my attitude was that of a fool. The impurities were embedded within me and dug deeper with every criminal decision I made.

Everybody took the most simple things for granted when behind bars. I missed having to wash dishes and mow the lawn. I missed simply just going outside whenever I wanted. I missed eating anything I desired and wearing whatever clothes I wanted to wear. You could buy stuff in prison, and I did, but I wasn't considered a rich man behind bars. The Natives were rich, big-time drug dealers were rich, and people who were experts in fields like electrical engineering, artistry, and woodworking were rich. There were guys in prison who would make so much money that they would send cash back to their families to fully support them. My mother would send me an allowance when I was young, and as I grew older, I made my own money, but I was far from wealthy. I took everything for granted until I had to provide for myself.

In prison, the economy was inflated. A honeybun cost $2 in the early 2000s. A virtual visit or video call could sometimes run you $30. A gram of weed cost $100 at the time. You could buy an ounce for $1500. Not a lot of dudes could afford the O, so whoever was able to, would sell it and use the profits to perpetually buy and sell weed. It was the same way with every other drug behind bars. Oxy, coke, heroin... If it was illegal, it was sold or traded. The dudes who did it at large-scale volumes would be considered rich out on the street. Those guys were few and far between, because they often had to work with corrupt guards who I did not have any relations with at that point. Brothers like me were able to move drugs through jail on a smaller, safer scale. I sold weed and tobacco, and it kept my pockets full enough to have the lifestyle I desired in incarceration. The way everyone saw it, I was a small businessman. I learned a lot about commerce, but my greatest acquisition of knowledge came on a hot summer's day about a year into my sentence.

The heat was sweltering in my cell. Star had taken off all his clothes but his underwear and he paced around the room like a maniac.

I sat on my bed with my back up against the wall and my radio in my hands. I could see heat waves dancing in the air before me. I fiddled with the knobs and buttons as the gentle but consistent echo of tapping of Star's bare feet was bouncing between all three walls. "Sit down, man," I yelled to him. Star stopped and looked at me. He had sweat running down his forehead and some of it was even dripping to the floor. "Fuck you," he responded, then switched on his soundless television and continued pacing back and forth as a newscaster inaudibly read the news.

I turned on my radio with a sigh. It was Sunday, and every Sunday at 5pm Pacific this local station would have a segment on sports called UP ON GAME. The two dudes who hosted the show were not only hilarious, but they provided a visceral description of sports games and plays from the week that had passed. I would always close my eyes and listen intently so that I would be able to visualize the words that came out of their mouths. They were natural-born orators, and I doubted that they knew a prisoner like me was their most disciplined listener.

"It ain't five yet," Star muttered to me as his eyes were glued to his silent television.

"I know, I'm just bored as fuck," I responded.

I twisted on the radio and a new rap song played suddenly. "Who is this?" Star asked. I had no idea. I just shrugged my shoulders. One thing about prison was that it always seemed like music on the street was surpassing you. Man, I was still listening to Tupac. All of that new shit sounded wrong. It sounded like it shouldn't have been music at all. Still, I listened to it and I internalized every word and beat. It was like sitting on the toilet and reading the informational patch on the back of a bottle of bleach. It was something to keep my mind from rotting. The music played and filled the cell with a beat until the sound of sizzling and static echoed. I slapped the radio with my strong hand and it went back to normal. I lay back to close my eyes and visualize the story that was being told to me when suddenly the entire thing crashed. The rapper's words faded into the darkness and as I opened my eyes I looked to my radio and fiddled with the knobs and buttons but nothing would work. My only form of entertainment in that fucking place had failed me.

"Motherfucker," I said as I tossed the faulty radio onto my pillow.

"You gotta take that shit to Antonio," Star said to me.

"Antonio?"

"Yeah, you know Antonio, the Mexican dude," he followed.

"The North Mexican dude?"

"The Norteño? Hell nah, fuck that motherfucker. He did me wrong. Antonio, the Southern dude. Sureño... You know, the guy who always wears earphones in the yard."

I knew who Star was talking about, but I didn't talk to him. I sold weed to a guy in the Northern Mexican gang, the Norteños, and out of respect I always kept my distance from the Sureños. We didn't have any other affiliation, but my boy spent five hundred bucks a month on my product and I couldn't lose that business. Those two gangs might have hated each other more than the Bloods and Crips. Tensions were always high and that was a fight I didn't need to jump into the middle of. Still, that was prison, and the laws of prison may not have been written, but they were known. When it came to business, you could trade between gangs and races. However, in the yard, a race riot could explode at any moment and you never knew who wanted to take advantage of it to beat your ass or kill your ass. People trained for those moments. The white dudes treated every morning the same a military man would. They did 88 push-ups, 88 sit-ups, and 88 burpees, every single day.

I walked through the yard looking for Antonio. I had my radio tucked into my waistband so that nobody would see it. I walked by the Bloods and got taunted heavily. I wanted to respond badly but my gang was over the other side of the yard. I had heard rumors that some of the Bloods had shanks hidden under the dirt in different areas of the yard so that if a fight did break out they could quickly dig them up and have the upper hand. The big dude in the front of the crew was called Chains. He was the most jacked of all of them. The Alpha. He had a harmonica in his tattooed hands. He never played that motherfucking thing, he just held it. It was bright and shiny and it was immaculately designed. It was clearly worth a lot of money and he was flaunting it like a peacock.

"Spivey," Chains yelled out to me.

I just kept walking. Chains laughed. I hated that fucking cackling laugh, but I valued the strategy of patience. If Chains made a move, I would have been ready. I was too smart to strike first. I could see Antonio sitting on some rafters amongst a group of Southern Mexican dudes. They all spoke to each other in Spanish. I could speak a little Espanol myself, but not at the speed at which they did. They spoke in tongues and the colloquialism of their dialogue made it impossible for even a native Spanish speaker to fully comprehend. You had to have been around these guys a lot to pick up on the information they were putting out.

"What the fuck do you want?" a voice yelled out from the Sureños.

"I need Antonio's help," I responded as I slowly revealed the radio in my waistband.

A few stood to their feet. They were riddled with Aztec tattoos that depicted violence and a higher power. They had Spanish words and Mexican mafia symbols imprinted on every visible part of their bodies. These men stood before me in menacing silence. I looked over their shoulders and saw that Antonio was bobbing his head with his earphones on. "My money's green, man," I said. The men cracked their knuckles and bounced on their feet. They were ready for something.

"We know who you are. We know you sell weed to the Norteños," one of them exclaimed.

"Business is business," I responded.

Antonio popped the headphones out from his ears and stood to his feet. He was small. He barely hit five foot-five with his shoes on. He pushed through the front line of his crew and stood before me by his lonesome. "What do you need?" he asked. He had a small mustache that somehow sat just above his lip and nowhere near his nose. His brown eyes were bloodshot and the number 13 was tattooed on his neck.

"My radio died. Can you fix it?" I said as I tossed him the device.

Antonio held the piece of junk in his hands. He inspected it closely with one eye closed. His coarse fingertips ran over the dials and buttons. "Five bucks and a fresh pair of sheets," he said without picking his head up. All of his boys were staring me down. Some sat, some stood tall. All of them are ready for anything, just as I was.

"Five bucks and a pair of sheets? That's expensive, man," I said.

"Then you can find another electrical engineer who can do it," Antonio responded as he put his headphones back in.

"Fine..."

I reached into my shoe and pulled out a five-dollar bill. It was crumbled and sweaty, but Antonio's eyes lit up when his dry fingertips grasped hold of the green tender. "I can have the sheets to you soon," I followed. Antonio nodded to me and retreated behind a wall of the massive Sureños. "No later than eight o'clock, you got that?". I understood completely. If Antonio fixed my radio and I did not pay him in full and on time, I could have woken up the next morning with a sharpened toothbrush sticking out of my abdomen.

I paced through the yard. I could see Star with his boys. He nodded to me indiscreetly. My crew was in sight by the bench press. Philly was pushing two-fifty while some of the other guys stood guard. He was a beast, and the veins in his biceps popped a colorful blue and red which was visible from the dozens of feet away I was. He was the alpha of our crew and I was a youngster. It was his duty to lead and he bore that responsibility selflessly. The eyes of every race and gang were burning a hole in my sides. Subsets of blacks wanted to kill me. The whites wanted to open me up and eat my liver raw. The Mexicans wanted to wrap a rope around my neck and dangle me before my own family. And, to my left, Xing and the Asians were playing cards. I walked by them and they paused. Xing watched every step I took through the dust and dirt. He sat next to a small black-haired dude with a homemade tattoo gun. All of those guys had Eastern tribal tattoos that were ripe and fresh with shades of red rashes glowing around the art.

"Spivey," Xing yelled out to me.

I turned and saw that he was walking toward me already with one hand in his pocket. I didn't know what was in there. I didn't have anything to defend myself with. I had a few bucks in my shoe but Xing sold swords and didn't need the payout. He was rich. "What were you doing with the Sureños?" He followed. I could see that his men were growing uneasy. The little Asian dude with the tattoo gun had placed it in the dirt and shoved his hand into his pocket.

"I paid for Antonio to fix my radio," I said.

Xing stood tall before me. He had close to six inches over me, and about fifty pounds, too. His jawline was square and chiseled and one strike against it would have broken my wrist. The man was a giant. I had heard that he was inside for triple homicide. He told the story with a self-defense spin, but you could see right through it. He caught his girl with another dude in his gang, so he killed them both, and the guy's roommate, too. I always understood that he murdered that last dude for shits and giggles. He was a fucked up individual when he turned that switch on, and there he was, squaring up to me in a yard filled with hundreds of motherfuckers who would have loved to have stabbed me.

"I need some tobacco, a lid's worth," Xing whispered.

"That it?"

"You toss in a gram of weed, I'll make you a sword," he followed.

Xing's swords were top-of-the-line. They were about eight inches from base to tip. They had a solid handle that was easy to keep your grip on, and the blade was sharp and could penetrate any part of the human body with minimal force. "Deal," I responded. Xing nodded to me and turned his back. His little Asian subordinate picked up his tattoo gun and blew the dust off it before turning it back on. The buzzing sound filled the air and as the tip of the gun touched the dry skin of Xing. A vibratory echo ran through my ears.

Yelling suddenly bellowed from across the yard. Anytime something like that happened, everyone would grow tense. In prison, if you had the time to react, you took every millisecond to prepare your body and mind. I turned and saw that Chains was screaming across the yard at Puma. "Yo Puma, listen to me, fool," Chains screamed. I wondered what it could have been about. I sauntered toward the conflict but made sure to keep my distance and watch my back. Everyone else was doing the same thing. They were watching, waiting, preparing for a riot to break out. I could even see that the guards were taking notice. A couple of them gently wrapped their gloved hands around their rifles.

"I'm talking to you, motherfucker," Chains yelled as he charged toward Puma.

Puma turned with a slight smirk on his face and a cigarillo buried between his chapped lips. His eyes were wide and filled with craze. He stood there by his lonesome with total nonchalance. Chains got right up in his face. He held his harmonica tightly in one hand as he turned his other hand into a fist. "I been hearing rumors about you," Chains said as he got right up close to Puma.

"I been hearin' rumors about you, too. I hear you like gettin' your asshole touched," Puma muttered with a devilish chuckle.

"You've been groping dudes in the shower, and now someone put a bounty on your head," Chains said with a smile.

"You think this is my first bounty? Bitch, every fuckin shade of skin has a bone to pick with Puma. But, you know what?"

"What?"

"Aint nobody ever done shit."

Puma spat on Chains' shoes. Chains looked all around and saw every pair of eyes watching him. He knew better than to shank that decrepit piece of shit. If he did, there were a hundred witnesses and he'd never have a chance to see the light of day again. He'd go in the box for a few months. Solitary confinement was no joke, and even the hardest motherfuckers like Chains knew that it was never worth it. If you wanted someone dead, you did that shit in silence.

"You're gonna find yourself in the infirmary with a motherfuckin' harmonica shoved up your ass if you ain't careful," Chains threatened.

Chains turned his back and threw up gang signs to his boys. They all laughed as he approached them, kicking up sand and dirt as Chains' booted shoes dug into the earth with every stomp toward them. "Yo Chains!" a yell suddenly screamed from the group. A giant veiny hand planted onto Chains' shoulder and spun him around violently. Chains' eyes shot wide open when he saw Puma swiftly remove his hand from his shoulder and turn it into a fist before landing a piledriver onto his face. Chains fell onto his back and a cloud of dust from the sand below fired up into the air and cast a wall of dusty smoke around the two men. A guard instantly shot a bullet high into the air and yelled "Nobody even think about fucking moving," over a microphone as several of his comrades rushed down to the yard in their riot gear.

Chains struggled on the ground as Puma weighed down on top of him. Puma ripped Chains' harmonica from his hand while his other hand pinned Chains' head to the dusty ground. "Is this the harmonica you was gonna shove up my ass?" He asked. Chains squirmed against the sandy surface and kicked his legs around in an attempt to push Puma off, but Puma was too strong. Puma took that harmonica and shoved it in Chains' mouth. Chains gagged and tears streamed from his eyes as Puma dug it deeper and deeper until a guard ran up right behind the rapist and dragged him off. Chains choked on the harmonica and his gasps for air emitted strange and off-kilter sounds from the instrument that was lodged in his throat. Another guard rushed to him and pulled the harmonica out from his esophagus. Drool and blood dripped from the once-shiny instrument and onto the yellow dirt below. "You're going in the box, Puma," one of the guards said before dragging his smiling ass away.

I was happy to leave the yard after that. We were all hardened criminals but violence was violence. It was always going to send a shiver up your spine and it was what you did with that feeling that defined you. Leaving the yard early gave me time to hit the laundry room. Star was working there at that moment and I knew that I could convince him to let a fresh sheet slide under the radar in exchange for some tobacco.

I paid off a guard that was stationed in the laundry room to let me enter for just five minutes. The guy's name was O'Bannion, and he was all right. He was fair and listened to what I said to him. I think he had as much respect for me as a prison guard possibly could for an inmate. It was because I was polite and I paid him whatever I could. That was the smart thing to do and I wasn't the only one who did it. Some of the guards made the bare minimum and had families to support at home just like a lot of us inmates. Hell, some of these dudes were even from the same neighborhoods as a lot of the inmates. The guys who gave the guards a hard time only shot themselves in the foot.

The laundry room had these massive blue washing machines and harsh gray dryer units stacked on top of each other that would viciously rumble with the force of the circulating interior. They stretched from wall to wall on either side of the room, and in the very center were long tables where inmates would fold the laundry and sort it into various piles to categorize the building, cells, and size of inmates. Star was folding some sheets when I walked in. "Yo Star," I said quietly. He turned to me and nodded in silence before returning to his duties. "I need a favor, bro," I followed. Star stopped folding and turned to me.

"You never do me any favors," he responded.

"Then, we won't call it a favor. I need a fresh pair of sheets, I'll trade you some tobacco for 'em," I said.

Star shook his head quietly. He resumed folding. I felt disrespected by my own cellie. I knew he didn't trust me as much as I didn't trust him, but in a few hours, we were going to be sitting five feet apart from each other. "What's your problem, man?" I asked. He sighed and set down the sheet. "I ask you questions all the time, man, and you just give me one-word answers," he muttered. "I don't like you because of that," he followed. I could feel the heat in the air get hotter. The day had been filled with so much chaos that I'd almost forgotten the sun's gruesome presence, and in that laundry room, we were boiling. Star wiped the sweat from his forehead with a sigh of frustration, then resumed his work.

"I promised Antonio I'd get him a fresh set in exchange for fixing the radio. If I don't have those sheets, the Sureños will put a target on my back," I said to him.

"Go back to the cell, Dave," he responded without even lifting his head.

A guard was standing at both doors in the room. One was for prisoners to enter, that's where O'Bannion was, and one was at the exit. I had no choice but to leave. O'Bannion was cool, but we agreed upon five minutes and I always stayed true to my word. "You could have just killed me yourself, motherfucker," I muttered as I left the laundry room.

Day fell into night and the sounds of inmates returning to their homes filled the hot air. I lay in my bed gazing up at the ceiling. I could feel the sweat on my back sticking to the dirty, dusty sheets that lay atop my inch-thick mattress. My fan was blasting at me from the foot of my bed and I could feel the cool air rushing between my toes. I closed my eyes and pictured being outside on a windy day. I remembered a time when my mom brought me and my brother to the beach. It wasn't a nice day, but my mother had made the promise and she always kept her word. The clouds were gray and populated the sky so we couldn't even see the sun. She sat on an old white sheet she had brought from home as my brother and I ran through the water that hit the shore and rose up the beach until it retreated back into the ocean. I remembered that on the way home we rolled down the windows and the cool air blasted against my salty face. I felt like I was being reborn.

"Spivey."

The time had come. I opened my eyes and Antonio was standing by the cell bars next to O'Bannion. He held the fixed radio in his hand. "Make it quick," O'Bannion said. I stood to my feet and sauntered toward the cell bars. I moved as slowly as I could, feeling the weight of consequence holding me back. When I reached the cell door, I looked at Antonio in his small, brown eyes.

"Where's the sheet?" he asked.

I sighed and counted the seconds before opening my mouth again. I knew that as soon as I told him, he would tuck that radio under his shirt and leave alongside O'Bannion. The next time I strayed from my gang, I was at risk of being attacked by a group of motherfuckers to whom I was indebted. That's just how prison worked. If you took, you had to give. If you couldn't give, somebody would take. There were a lot of rules in prison, and all of them weighed about equal, but if somebody did something for you, you were required to have the respect to get them back.

"Star Jones, welcome home," O'Bannion said out of the blue as he turned his head.

Star stepped into sight. My eyes grew wide and a smile pleasantly struck my face. In his hands was a fresh sheet all folded up and smelling nice. It had the stench of a loving mother's laundry. "Here you go," Star said as he handed the sheet to Antonio and received the repaired radio in return. Antonio stuck his hand through the cell bars and extended it to me. I shook it. "No more selling weed to the Norteños," he said. I nodded to him. That was an agreement, not just a transaction. By staying cool with Antonio, I could have anything I wanted to be fixed within a day. My northern boy was just going to have to find some other place to buy his weed. Star lay down on his bed and gazed up at the ceiling. We both sat there in silence as the fan spun and blew air onto my body. "Thanks," I said. "I appreciate you," I followed. Star planted the souls of his feet onto the sizzling surface of the cell floor. I perked up and did the same.

"You and I met once, you know. We were at the same cantina on Crenshaw," Star said.

"Esmerelda's?"

"Yeah, a few years ago. You were with a woman, so was I. They knew each other and introduced us," Star explained with a smile.

"Oh man, I do remember that," I said with wide eyes.

"You ever still talk to that chick?" Star asked.

"Nah, man. That was a one-and-done. My momma didn't like her one bit," I said before both of us broke into laughter.

I turned on my radio and we lay in silence listening to music for hours that night. Every day afterward became a little more bearable with him there. I had finally trusted Star and I knew that he had finally developed some trust for me. The greatest acquisition of knowledge came to me that day. Everybody is a fucking expert, and you have to navigate your way through it all. You have to know what you bring to the table, and in prison, I brought loyalty and drugs. I learned it was a helpful mix that would get me where I needed to be to stay safe there, at least in the beginning. I had made new friends, but in doing so, I had created enemies. There was no such thing as universal love, and I would pay for it.

Incubus

My cell is dark and filled with shadows. The air is cold and steam emits from my mouth as I exhale. My eyes are bloodshot and I experience a sharp pain in them that I cannot describe. I look at my forearms and the red and blue veins run along my skin like rivers on a map. My hands shake violently and sweat perspires on my forehead and runs down to my trembling lips. "Star," I say with a rumble in my voice. There is no response. His cot is empty and neatly dressed. I sit up in my bed and plant the souls of my feet on the floor. The concrete is cold as ice and it sends a shiver up my spine and pops goosebumps out from my dry skin. I feel a stream of cold air running down from the ceiling and onto my neck. I cringe and roll my shoulders forward, squirming as I jump to my feet and pace around my room. Everything is incredibly silent. There are no yells, coughs, snores, or sounds of any kind inside or outside the room. I grab my radio and as I twist the dial the button breaks free from the device and I hold it in my trembling hand. "Motherfucker," I mumble. I carefully place the broken part onto my bed, then I gently wrap the tips of my index finger and thumb around the other dial. I gently spin the piece of metal. Clicking noises emit from the moving part and suddenly the entire device crumbles to thousands of tiny shards right in the palm of my hands. My wide eyes gaze down at the metal shavings. My arms shake as I lift them to my mouth and blow the ashes into the air. They hang in suspension for a moment before fluttering down to the cold floor. The television sparks alive while my back faces the screen and I slowly turn to it. The entire window is red and casts an ominous maroon light onto me. Shadows imprint onto the plain wall behind me. The scarlet illumination creates moving blobs of light along my black skin. Patches of darkness and light shift along my body and turn my corneas into infrared goggles.

"What the fuck is happening?" I say as my wet fingertips slide along my plump forearms.

A slither of smoke streams through the air and hangs beneath my nose. It smells like weed and tobacco, a spliff. The corner of the room lies in complete and utter darkness. The smoke runs in a line from within the darkness and directly to me. I take one step forward when a glowing, crackling ember of a pipe gently illuminates from within the night. The gentle light reveals a pitch-black hand wrapped around the base of a wooden pipe and the lower half of a face with no features. It's a dark silhouette sitting there and taunting me and I'm paralyzed from its presence. My feet won't move closer to it nor will it allow me to retreat backward. My body trembles and shakes as my eyes are locked on the sizzling and glowing embers of sparkling crackles of weed and tobacco.

"Who are you?" I mumble.

The sizzling embers within the crackling pipe fade back into darkness and I can move my legs once more. I lean on the tips of my toes. I can feel the shadow's presence lingering around me when suddenly the echo of creaking bones fills the air. A pair of glowing yellow eyes open from within the corner of darkness and the figure stands tall, high above my eye-line. I lift my head toward the ceiling to stare into them and the lemon lenses are wide and unforgiving. They stare right back at me with no intention of shifting their gaze. I back up into the bars of my cell door and my lungs fill with air, nearing the point of popping like a balloon. The silhouette breathes harshly and heavily. I can feel the wind blow from its nostrils and onto my face. It smells wretched and the air is colder than the floor that freezes the souls of my feet.

"What do you want?"

The creature's bones creak as the silhouette takes a step toward me. Its entire body still remains in darkness but I can feel it shifting slowly as the menacing pair of yellow eyes stare at me with a clear sting burning within them. A growl rumbles from within the darkness and I turn to face the door. I grip my hands around two of the cell bars and I violently pull back and forth. The metal shakes. The noise of the shifting beast behind me grows louder as its bones snap in and out of place with every minor step. The bars miraculously snap in half and I hold the two beams in my trembling hands. I drop them to the floor and jump into the cell door with my entire weight. I come crashing through the bars and land on the floor just outside my cell. I lay on the cold ground gazing through the man-sized gap and from within it I hear the rumble of deep, demonic laughter that echoes through the entire block. I push myself to my feet and limp as fast as I can down the hallway. I peer over the ledge of the third floor and look to the ground twenty feet below. It's pitch black and I can't make out the definition of a single item. As I limp by cell after cell I notice that each one is uninhabited and filled with darkness. The sound of my feet tapping against the metal lingers in the air with an echo as I trudge further and further from my home. I look over my shoulder as I shimmy along the rail and the darkness follows me, eating up everything that is cast in light and removing it from existence.

I don't see the staircase coming and I fall right down it with a thud. I smash my head off every other step and when I roll to the bottom I can feel blood seeping through strands of my hair. I vibrate as I attempt to push myself to my feet but my arms give in and I fall face-first onto the cold concrete below. "Come on, Dave," I mumble. Things like this only happen to people who deserve it.

The menacing laughter returns and as I lay on the ground I flip onto my back to gaze upward at the metal staircase. At first, I can see the top step but after a moment the darkness rolls over and begins to remove everything from existence. The blackness falls gently down the stairs and comes right at me. A rumble of menacing laughter comes from within the unknown and shakes the prison. Dust falls from the ceiling and hangs in the air like glistening snowflakes in the moonlight on a dark winter night. I keep pushing and pushing myself but my arms are growing tired and weak. I look forward and see the exit door to the yard. It's only twenty-five feet away. I whip my neck around and see that the darkness has engulfed the entire staircase and the sound of creaking bones lingers in the air. I can hear every painful step the silhouette makes and suddenly from within the darkness, I spot its yellow eyes once more. They are clandestine and filled with terror.

My dry, chapped hand wraps around the cool, steel handle of the door. I pull myself to my feet and I almost fall right back down. My legs feel like spaghetti. It's as if every step I take, I grow weaker. I rattle the door knob but the door will not open. The creaking echo of snapping bones and snarling laughter ripples through the air as the dust continues to flutter down from the ceiling above. Darkness has eaten all of the light. I stand in the only illumination of my dreams and

I pull and pull on the escape. I look through the window in the door and gaze out to the yard. The moon hangs high in the sky and casts a ray of gentle light onto the sand. I squint. There's someone out there, way in the distance. They wear black. Smoke and steam surround them in a motion of ecstasy as they walk toward me. I've seen this person before. They have that familiar aura about them but I cannot make out who it is under this kind of pressure. I bang on the glass but it will not break. "Help me, help," I yell as the door ruptures in place with every fierce blow I make to its viewing glass.

"David," the creature's voice rumbles deeply through the air.

I close my fist and smash it off the window over and over. My fingers and knuckles start to bleed and blood drips to my bare feet below. I turn and the darkness is but ten feet from my trembling and aching body and all I want more than anything is to break free. This fucking door is constructed from obsidian and no tool in existence can penetrate its structure. "Help me, for God's sake," I scream with tears in my eyes. The figure steps into the moonlight and I drop my bloody hands down by my sides. The dripping sound echoes every second but my gaze to the yard is unbroken. Standing in the moonlight is my mother. She's wearing all black and her dress waves in the wind that circulates the steam and smoke around her. My breathing slows down and I can feel my heart thumping through my chest. "Mom," I mutter. My bloody hands shake and my lips tremble. Tears rush down my face and my knees rumble violently. I'm falling apart and the only person who can put me back together is her.

"Mom!"

She steps right before the glass and just stares at me. I look like a child. My eyes are red and I sniffle with every sharp breath. I place my hand on the glass and spread my fingers apart. She just stares right back at me with dead eyes. I can feel the air grow cold and as I look down to my feet I see a layer of darkness sweep in like waves on a beach. "Mom, please," I say to her as the blackness gently wraps itself around my shins and gradually moves up my legs. I feel my toes and ankles wither away from existence and my mom just stands there watching it happen with dry eyes. I bang on the glass once more but nothing happens. "I'm sorry, Mom," I whisper as the darkness wraps itself around my waist. I drop my gaze to my feet and I see the unknown swallowing me whole. I close my eyes with a sting.

"You're not going anywhere," the creature's voice deeply echoes.

I open my eyes and before me is a pair of yellow lenses peering into my soul. They are inches from my face. I can feel the cold wind from the exhales of the beast blow wretched smells into my nostrils. I can barely make out the creature's body by its slithering silhouette in the darkness. It mocks me as it takes its thin and scaled finger and rubs it along my cheek. It has black nails that are cracked and browned under the fingertips. "Mom," I whisper as the creature opens its hand wide and spreads its fingers out like a fan. It places its palm on my quivering face and everything goes dark. All that's left is my conscience and the realization that I am going to die in prison and there's nothing anybody can do about it. The creature has embedded itself into my soul and is pulling the strings of my wretched existence until the day I am put down like the dog that I am.

Getting Out of the Hole

The darkness of my dreams were consuming my mind every hour of the day. I was becoming more on edge as time went on. Artificial light that shone through the bars of my cell illuminated the room and cast sparkling rays onto the homemade sword that I held in my hands. Star and I sat on my bed and admired the weapon. It was constructed from various pieces of metal like coat hangers and old spoons. I didn't fully understand how Xing did it, but I do know that he reconstructed a hot plate in his cell so that it would burn twice as hot and mold metal twice as fast. On the outside, he was somewhat of a blacksmith. He was supposedly a gifted student but he quit high school and tried setting up his own welding business, both to his family's dismay. Like the rest of us, he got caught up in some shit and all of it went down the drain. In prison, he was a weapons expert, and that provided him a good living. Not every dude in that place had a knife as I did, so if anything went down, I would be ready.

"Can you believe we've been in here for a year and a half?" Star said.

"Only have the rest of my life to go," I responded.

I slid the sword under my pillow and stood to my feet to stretch out wide. It was morning time and I was still tired. I needed to go outside and move my legs so that my mind would wake up. My pockets were full of tobacco and weed in little plastic bags. I decided I would roll something up for the yard. It was over a hundred degrees outside and I didn't want to kick dust without something illicit running through my veins.

"Roll for two," Star said as he perked up.

I rolled two spliffs and handed one to Star. We sat in silence as the heat hung in the air. There was commotion outside the cell but nothing out of the ordinary. We could hear dudes yelling and screaming at the top of their lungs. It was like elementary school in the way that the immature inmates would compete for being the loudest and most obnoxious. Some guys just wanted to create chaos in every aspect of their lives. The guards didn't like fellas like that. Neither did I, but I wasn't about to start anything. Tensions had been boiling to a bubble in the previous months and we had gone almost ninety days without any sort of riot in the yard.

"You hear Puma's getting out of the box today?" Star said.

"You're kiddin'," I responded.

Puma had spent months in solitary confinement for what he did to Chains. That dude had closed the door to parole a long time ago. I was surprised he wasn't moved to protective custody. At that moment, I still had another eleven years until I was even eligible for parole. It wasn't a thought in my mind. In prison, you had to always stay focused on the present because you never knew what was right around the corner.

"Can I ask you something, man?" Star said to me.

"Sure."

"You ever thought about getting your degree?"

"Nah, man. You see the dudes who do it... They're still here, man. Their degree does nothing for them."

"Those guys get in trouble for doing the same bad shit we do... I'm just saying that it would be nice to focus on something else for a change..."

A lot of guys got a degree or a diploma in prison. For the dudes that were going to be released within their lifetime, it made sense, as long as they had the discipline to walk the fine line to freedom. For a brother like me, it was a waste. I was a smart person and I had a lot of knowledge but most of it pertained to people and why they acted the way they did. I valued that skill on the street just as much as I did in prison. I knew when it was cool to talk to someone and when it wasn't.

"Dave," a voice bellowed.

Tippeconnic stood outside my cell. He was the alpha of the Native American crew. He was tight with the guards and we often saw him walking around the third floor handing people books. He had these crazy tribal tattoos and long, black hair that fell below his shoulder blades. He read a lot, too. Tippeconnic was a smart motherfucker and he was the right man to delegate literature within those walls. That was a good job in prison because you got to move around and see what everyone was up to. You could view the entirety of the place in real-time as opposed to hearing about stories and events in hindsight. The Native Americans were guys that you really only spoke to about drugs and money, nothing else. I knew that if I crossed that line, they would just pay some motherfucker in a rival gang to shank me. Everything was a fine line and I was a fucking trapeze artist balancing on that shit like a pro. I was a guy who people tolerated and respected and in prison that was as good as you could get.

"You got any weed?" Tippeconnic asked.

"I got a couple g's. I'll have more next week," I responded.

"I will take what you have now," he said as he handed me five, one hundred dollar bills rolled up into a cylinder.

Nobody did more drugs than the natives. They had money to blow. If you ever saw Tippeconnic or one of his dudes in the yard, there was a one-hundred percent chance that they were high on something. Heroin, weed, cocaine, oxy, Xanax, ketamine... It did not matter. As long as their mind was not present in prison they could survive. All of us other inmates wished we could have done the same thing. Nobody had the sauce to do that shit. I'm sure the clean-cut guards knew how narcotics were coming in but those dudes didn't make a whole lot of money so sometimes it simply wasn't worth their while cracking down on us small-time prison dealers. All I had to do was not fuck up or piss any of them off and I could keep pushing how I had been pushing since I bought my first ounce.

Tippeconnic vanished and O'Bannion showed his freckled face. It was time to go to the yard. "Dave, Star, let's go," he said as he swung our cell door open. We all walked in a straight line down the metal staircase and out to the yard. O'Bannion walked right behind us. "How's your kids?" I asked. "Good, the little one is starting school in a couple weeks," he responded. O'Bannion was a good man. I knew little about him but that was only because he tried to keep his distance as much as possible. We all tried to.

When I stepped foot outside the sun blasted me with a hot ray of light that burned my corneas. I lifted my arm to shade my face. My vision was blurred for a moment until my eyes adjusted to the light and I could see everyone. I walked alongside Star until he saw some dudes from his old neighborhood and he joined them. I threw up my hand as a symbol of peace and I received some love in return. I didn't know any of Star's boys that well but we were all cut from the same cloth.

"Yo Dave," Philly yelled from a bench.

I approached my gang and I bounced from homie to homie, shaking hands and cracking jokes. Philly was in a great mood that day. He was always pretty level-headed and never showed too much emotion, exactly how a general should be. He was tightly wound but a caring individual all the same. Nobody really knew anything about him and he liked it that way, but on that day he had a smile on his face and positive vibes exerting out into the world. "I don't know how it happened, but I got approved for parole, man. I showed them what kind of dude I had become and they saw the real me and not my crimes. In 120 days, imma' be out of here," Philly exclaimed. He had already spent quite some time in prison and had been denied parole on several occasions. I didn't think he'd ever get it but Philly grew smart with age. He had his boys' backs but he never initiated anything because he knew that those who did would never be able to leave. Being in a gang in prison is all about loyalty. It's all we had and if one of our brothers needed our help we had no choice but to aid them in whatever danger was afoot. It was a fine line that few knew how to navigate effectively, and by effectively it meant doing it so discreetly that your record stayed clean. Back then, I certainly didn't realize what it would take. If the wrong guard knew that I sold weed and tobacco, they could put it on my file and when my parole would roll around it would be the first thing that they saw.

"The first thing I'm gonna' do, man, is fuck my old bitch," Philly said with wide eyes and a smile on his face.

"You think she still gives a fuck about you? She's probably married, bro. How long's it been?"

"I don't give a fuck. That was my girl and when I get out she's gonna' be mine again," Philly responded.

That day started out as a good day. Every gang was adequately segregated and there wasn't a hint of tension in the air. Everyone was just going about their own business. Those days made you feel like prison was normal. You ate vending machine food and smoked cigarettes and weed and the sun hung high in the air just like it used to when we were kids. We were all joking around and pushing each other into the dirt like motherfuckers at recess. I had never seen Philly so giddy. He was a general who acted like a rookie. You would have never believed that the man was a cold-blooded killer. Everything made him laugh that day and it rubbed off on everyone else. I wished that that feeling would have lingered just a little bit longer.

"Philly, look..."

Philly turned his head and the smile was instantly wiped from his face. We all stood there like lemurs watching lions pass in the open plains of Africa. Before us was Puma, and he looked disheveled, thin, and mad. He spun a cigarette around his fingers and licked his lips as he strolled by gang after gang like a jungle cat. Xing and the Asians watched every step he took. Antonio removed his headphones and shoved his hand in his pocket to grab the knife that was pressing up against his spleen. The natives were sitting on the rafters and when they saw Puma they moved to a different side of the yard and had two white men with Arian tattoos guard them. "He's back," a voice bellowed from my gang. My eyes followed that motherfucking rapist as he took calm and gentle steps through the dust and sand. Everybody grew tense and the heat from the sun suddenly became cool.

"I hate that motherfucker," Philly said. "Someone oughta stab that piece of shit," he followed.

I watched as Puma continued to walk through the yard. He turned the heads of every single inmate and guard. He was heading right for the Bloods, right for Chains. They saw Puma approaching from a mile away and they were ready. I could see a couple of them crouching close to the dirt. My immediate thought was, *"That must be where the knives are dug."* Most of them stood tall with their arms crossed and their chests puffed out. Chains had his shirt off. He stretched his muscles and shook his arms to get loose for battle. I looked around at the guards watching down on us from above and even though they wore thick sunglasses, I could tell that their eyeballs were jumping between Chains and Puma as they did not know who would draw first. None of us did.

"I'm in here for life, motherfucker. You know what that means?" Chains yelled.

"Nah," Puma mumbled as he trudged toward Chains, who stood in front of his gang of cold-blooded killers with his arms thrown out wide. I knew right then that I should have brought my sword. "It means I'll kill a motherfucker and my life won't change one bit," Chains said as he took one step toward Puma.

The yard dulled to a chilling silence as the sharp sound of a slash pierced through the air. Puma stood before Chains with a painted shiv in his bloody hand, which dripped red to the dirt below. The blood stained the ground and pooled at the feet of the knife wielder. Chains' arms shook violently as he touched his own wound on his bare torso. Life spilled out from the perforated blow and drained right into the puddle. Chains' eyes flickered as they rose to meet Puma's. His lips trembled and I could tell he wanted more than anything to speak one last time but the gravity of death blew out the back of his legs and he crumbled to the dirt. Smoke kicked up in the air and moved along with the wind as Puma stood tall with the stained weapon dripping by his side.

A gunshot exploded and a bullet whizzed up high into the sky with smoke and flash bursting through the barrel of O'Bannion's gun. "Everybody lie on their fucking stomachs right now," O'Bannion yelled at the top of his lungs. The Bloods didn't listen. They dug up their weapons and charged at Puma who turned and sprinted in my direction. Sand and dirt were being kicked up into the air and inmates were falling over Chains' lifeless body. Everybody saw that as their chance to take out rivals. "Stay smart," Philly said to us.

We stood our ground and kept our heads on a swivel as we watched the Norteños jump the Sureños. Antonio had removed a blade from his pocket and his headphones dangled down by the dirt as he waved away two of his rivals. "Cabrón," they yelled as Antonio swatted them away. One of the Norteños grabbed Antonio from behind and the shiv fell into the dirt. He put Antonio into a headlock and kept him in place through the struggle. I watched as they picked up his knife and stuck it back in him before letting him go and watching him fall face-first into the sand. Then, I saw some other Norteños turn to look at me. They knew who I was and they knew that the reason I stopped selling weed and tobacco to them was because of my relationship with Antonio. Three of them walked toward me. It was Rafael, Miguel, and Tomas. My fists were clenched and I was ready to fight.

"You see them Mexicans heading this way?" Philly said to me.

"Yeah," I responded quietly.

The guards were rushing down to the yard and I knew that in sixty seconds or less, we would have all been laying face first in the dirt with our hands stretched out wide. All I had to do was fend off those motherfuckers long enough for nothing to happen. If I did the wrong thing, my life sentence could become even more imprinted on my soul. I had been having enough nightmares as it was. They had been eating me alive and I had been jolting awake in the middle of the night covered in sweat with the feeling of iron in my lungs. Prison was not the place to express yourself or talk about things like that. The only time a brother was allowed to cry was when somebody in his family died. If you showed weakness you were done for, and I would never have expressed that back then. I was a rock and if those motherfuckers wanted to fight me for breaking our little piece of trust then that's what I was prepared for. I had done them wrong for doing business with their enemies and I was going to face the consequences like a man.

Philly stood in front of me and punched Rafael right across his fat face and he went crashing into the dirt with a thud. Dust flew into the air as Philly stood over the collapsed body while Tomas and Miguel faced off with him on the other side of their fallen friend. Another gunshot echoed across the yard as the guards rushed to the perimeters of the court. Miguel jumped at Philly but Philly was able to grab him and they wrestled to the ground. Tomas sprinted at me and swung a punch but I dodged it and lifted my fists once more. I kicked toward him and swung a blow but Tomas dodged it with ease.

"You little fuckin' bitch," Philly yelled as he got on top of Miguel and punched him over and over.

The sounds and yells of aggression distracted me long enough for Tomas to punch me square across my jaw and I fell to the ground in a daze. I gazed up at the blistering hot sun and its rays filled my eyes with light. Blood spilled from my nose. Tomas stood in front of the beaming beauty and darkness cast over me. He lifted his leg to stomp on my face when a rubber bullet caught him in the chest and he fell to the dirt wheezing. "Get on your fucking stomach," a yell bellowed from the commotion. I flipped over and threw my arms out wide by my side. I scanned the yard and dust and smoke hung in the air as guards were blasting rubber bullets at inmates covered in blood. There were bodies all about and they were barely filled with enough life to keep living. Some looked to be dead. Some looked to be dying.

"You like that, motherfucker?"

I turned left and saw that Philly was still on top of Rafael. His fists were as red as the devil's blood itself. His eyes were filled with rage and fury and as O'Bannion came tackling him to the ground I knew that Philly would never get approved for parole again in his life. All he had to do was make it 120 days without being reprimanded and it took no time at all for it all to just go away.

As the air blew the smoke and dust away I could finally get a good look at the whole yard. Puma lay in a pool of his own blood but he was still smiling. His teeth had been painted red and his eyes had big fat veins popping out of them like somebody stuck his head in the microwave. His right arm would flinch every other moment but other than that he could hardly move. My gaze drifted and I found Star to be okay and lying on his stomach just like I was. He stared directly into my eyes and I could tell we were both happy to see each other okay. Some of Star's brothers were being pinned down by the guards for beating the shit out of some white men. Xing also lay on his stomach with his arms down by his side. He was too smart to get caught. I never did find out if he killed anyone during that riot. I knew he had a sword on him but I did not know where it went or where he could have hidden it. What I did know was that there were five different dudes that never came back to their cells that day. Antonio was sliced by the Norteños, Chains was perforated by Puma, and the other three had been skewered by something only Xing could have made and concealed.

Philly was denied parole. It was after that riot that I put my first transfer notice in and within no time at all I was shipped out of the desert and taken to Northern California. Geography didn't matter. Prison was always going to be a prison, but when blood was spilled like that it was a sign that there could be more life elsewhere. I was a cold motherfucker on the streets but I had a brain and I was listening to it. To everyone else, I was a gangster. I was a killer and I was loyal. I sold drugs and I loved women. I left my brother Star behind in that chilling place and I told him that we would see each other again, whether it was out on the streets, or behind bars. He was the only piece of me that stayed behind in the desert and the only true lasting memory I have of that place that I think fondly of. Little did I know that my next institution would prove to be the most hostile environment I had ever experienced. Tensions were high 24 hours a day, even when you were sleeping. It was where I experienced the deadliest nightmares of my existence.

Days of Movement

The highway stretched for miles. The sun had already set over the mountains of sand and stone in the Southern California desert. All that remained was the ember light that illuminated the sky in a pink and purple hue. If I leaned closer to the bus window and gazed directly upward I could see the moon growing brighter by the second. It stood alone in the clear sky. My gaze lingered on it until the sky turned dark and starry friends accompanied the orbiting moon with a sparkle. I was finally leaving the desert behind for greener pastures.

The bus ride was eleven hours long and we rode through the night. I don't know why we did it that late, but I wasn't complaining. The other inmates that were being transported to the same institution were all asleep. For some of them, it looked like the first time they were hitting R.E.M since the day they were incarcerated. For me, I saw it as a chance to reconnect with the outside world, even for a short while. We first rode through desert towns that were all situated along the banks of the highway. Their buildings were old and withered from the California climate but they stood tall and firm and boasted a rich Wild West history. The rest of it was sand and dust, just like the yard. I imagined myself stranded alone in these parts with no food or water and solely having the desire to return home. I thought to myself that I would make it no matter what, but my gaze stopped at the desert horizon and who knew what lay beyond it.

I had forged a relationship with the desert heat. I became familiar with the sun and the rays it laid down upon me from above. The burning sensation of light that stained my skin with sunspots was a feeling I had thought would linger for a lifetime. The Sierra Nevada mountain range changed all that for me. After having only seen a flat desert for so long, seeing those peaks and rocky edges that rose high into the air made me feel small in the world. There were patches of pearl-white snow that covered the craggy peaks of the mountains like a blanket. Little green patches of grass popped up along the edges of the road and ran all the way up to the base of the mountain range. In every other bush, a flower would pop its colors like a light in the night.

"Can I open a window, boss?" one of the inmates asked the guard.

"Sure," the guard responded with one eye closed.

A stream of warm air ran through the bus and circumnavigated around the vehicle. I felt the wind rush between my ears and through strands of my hair. Goosebumps popped out from my arms and I just lay back and closed my eyes for a brief moment. I felt like I could breathe. It really seemed like that was the moment I was leaving prison for good, but that feeling was quickly dashed when another inmate piped up and said, "How about me, boss?". The guard reminded everyone that it was no school trip. He hammered the stake of justice right back into our hearts and left us to sit in pain. I returned my gaze to the window and as I looked out to the mountain range that was both vastly approaching yet still so far away, I saw a crack of lightning spray across the night sky and light the white tips in the grand painting before me. The hot desert air seemed to exhaust and what took its place was cool and chilling.

I could hear the thunder, and I could feel the wind. The yellow landscape of the California desert was now green and spanning with emerald bushes and trees that sparsely lined the landscape until they completely overtook it. The sky lit up every other moment with a flash and revealed to us our new climate. The wind would cause a creak in the bus windows with its force. The driver tightened his grip on the wheel slightly more and kept us on our straight and narrow.

The evergreen trees were tall and thick. They looked to have stood the test of time, perpetually forced to stay in the one spot for eternity. The moonlight cast its shadows onto the highway as we rode on and the silhouettes of their leaves and thistles would run along my face as my eyes followed the motion of the bus. When you're in prison, it feels like you're stagnant. You don't feel the passage of time and aging is nothing more than a surprise. It was difficult to feel change when that was how you perceived life.

Psychical movement altered that thought. When I was on that bus, going 80 or 90 miles per hour, seeing all of the trees, mountains, hills, bushes, grass, and animals, I could feel the change. I understood the concept of time and how it was passing by. I wanted to reach out and grab something just to know it was all still real. I knew I couldn't. I knew that I was strapped into my seat and would be held there for the rest of my days.

The propulsion of the vehicle made me think about my future. I thought about where I would be as an old man. If I stayed on that path, I would rightfully still be behind bars. A man who wanted change but did nothing to allow himself to change was somebody who would grow frustrated with his situation. I was afraid of being one of those guys. I knew that proper change came from discipline but as a young man only a couple years into his life sentence, I had yet to fully realize that. When the light from the illuminated sky above flashed onto my wide-eyed face, I could feel the optimism that so many strived to feel.

"Five minutes, everyone. Make sure you're awake and ready," the guard bellowed.

The skies became calm once more and the sun's light crept into the air. Everybody asleep arose just in time to watch the rays pop out over the evergreen trees and reveal the golden sky from within the sparkling night. An ember and orange hue glowed and the interior of the bus became warm once more. The guard stood tall and walked along the aisle to ensure we were all still in chains and ready for deployment into the institution. I could see the bus driver struggling to stay awake yet his coarse hands were still gripped around the leather wheel of this mechanical beast.

"Damn," a mumble came from a white man at the back of the bus.

The walls of the institution came into sight and they stretched higher than the tips of the evergreen trees that surrounded the landscape for miles and miles. I heard birds chirping and leaves rustling in the cool, Northern California air. The wheels of the bus creaked as they slowed to a halt at the entrance of the prison and exhaust rushed up the sides of the bus and blocked the view from the windows. I kept my gaze stationary as the steam rolled along the glass. The bus began moving and the wall of fog vanished only to reveal that we were inside the walls of our new home and it looked no different from my previous quarters in the desert. Everything was the same.

I stepped off that bus with shackles around my ankles and handcuffs on my wrists. I took a deep breath and took one step forward in a line of other inmates. We were silent and tired after our journey but we knew that once we walked inside and set up shop in our new home, we would likely all never speak again unless it was for business purposes. With every forward movement toward that jailhouse, I thought about my mother and how she was hundreds of miles from where I was. I thought about my little brother who was a teenager and following my path. I could feel their hearts beating for me and I knew there was nothing I could say that would make them respect who I had become. My brother had no other choice like me, but my momma felt that both of us were worth saving. The period of my life in that institution would prove to be the hardest challenge I ever faced. I wanted to claw my way through the gravel and stone to crawl back home to Inglewood and wrap my arms around my mom and brother. Yet, I was stationary, and my mind soon began to wander into nightmarish territories where it seemed like it would never return.

The Gym

The orange jumpsuit covering my skin was poorly washed and slightly tattered. A little hole with blackened burn marks surrounding the circle's edge was visible on the sleeve. The previous inmate to have worn it must have burnt a cigarette out on his arm. The suit was tight to my crotch and when I scratched the pinned area I could feel the threading of the material coming apart. Sweat caused that. A lot of dudes in Southern California had that problem, especially during the summer. I had never been to Northern California by that point in my life and I honestly didn't know much about it other than it was a hell of a lot colder than where I was from.

All of us new inmates stood in a line before a booth as we awaited to find out where our bunks would be and who they would be with. No California prison would ever house inmates that had opposing ideologies and loyalties in the same cell. That happened before, and motherfuckers died. It was a no-brainer, but for some folk, it didn't cross their mind. I knew I was going to be okay, as long as my cellie wasn't a dude like Puma. The guys who got paired with a rapist either tacked years onto their sentence for beating their cellie to a pulp, or they were raped and scarred for life.

"Next," the guard in the booth yelled.

I stepped up and laid a dead gaze upon the guard behind the thick panel of glass before me. "Name," she mumbled without lifting her head. She sat on an old, spinning office chair that was too low to the ground. The adjuster was snapped in half. She had to slightly lean when she typed onto the computer on her desk.

"Dave Spivey," I said.

"You mean David?" she responded quickly.

"David, yeah."

"Use the name your momma' gave you, son," she said as she clicked a button on her keyboard.

Her eyes flickered as the computer stalled while searching for my name. She lifted her eyes slightly to meet my gaze and I finally got a good look at her face. She wore glasses and was around the age of my own mother but she had gray, tethered hair like a bundle of fishing lines. She gave off an energy that I hadn't felt since I was last by my mom's side.

"Looks like you're in the Gym," she said as she took off her glasses.

"The Gym? Like a gymnasium?"

"This prison is overcrowded, son. This is how we have to do it. Now, step into that line over there and a guard will take you over shortly," she responded.

I stood amongst an even smaller group of inmates and we all watched as the remainder of the fresh batch were taken to their cells. Meanwhile, the rest of us were waiting in silence, unsure about what we were about to walk into. "Y'all heard of the Gym before?" A white inmate in the group muttered. Nobody responded. Hardly any of us even lifted our heads. Some of us were clearly first-timers. You could spot them from a mile away.

"If what I heard is true, then we're all in for it," the white man followed.

"Shut the fuck up, man," a Mexican man from the group yelled out.

Two guards with pistols holstered in by their sides walked before our group. They led us through a set of doors and down a dark hallway with light sparingly laid out every so often that a beam of artificial rays blasted you for a split second before you entered the darkness once again. The tunnel felt perpetual and never-ending. The thought of whatever was on the other side lingered in all of our minds. The guards stopped ahead of us. One of them approached a door and the other stood before our group and held his right hand out to stop us. The gateway slowly opened and rays of light began to shine in. The illumination crept along the floor as the Gym revealed itself with every movement of the door. The light rose up my orange jumpsuit and struck me in the eyes. I had to blink and slowly lift my lids to adjust my sight.

"Come on," one of the guards yelled.

I could hear the echoed chatter of inmates coming from within the Gym. The noises grew louder until I stepped through the doorway and witnessed what I knew would be the worst living situation of my prison life. The Gym was about the size of a college gymnasium. Bunk beds spanned across the vast space and were placed in proximity to one another. I could see that pockets of the Gym were occupied by specific races, and they were all represented, just like they were at my last institution. The realization came to me immediately. If I were bunked in the wrong part of the room, there was a good chance that I wouldn't even survive the night. My beliefs and loyalty to my gang were pungent, and as I was led by a guard along pockets of men in rival gangs and races, I could tell that they were dreaming of the moment I would screw up so they could get me.

"Spivey, you're here," the guard yelled.

The guard pointed at an open bed in the center of the Gym. There were three men on three different beds and the open spot was the bottom bunk on my right-hand side. I approached them and they all turned to look at me. Silently, I placed my belongings on my bunk and I sat on the mattress. It was thin and felt like it was made of rubber, but I knew I could get used to it. I cracked my knuckles together and stared at my hands, spotting the ground through the gaps between my fingers. One of the inmates in my pocket jumped off his bed and stood before me with his arm extended and held inches from my face.

"Yo' man, I'm Eric, this is Joe," he said and pointed at Joe on the top bunk with his hands behind his head.

I lifted my head and saw that Eric had his hand extended before me. There were tattoos riddled along his arm and as I looked at his face I saw familiar imprints on his neck and cheeks. He resembled people from my neighborhood. He and I were in the same gang. We probably knew some of the same people, but Eric looked like he was older. "I'm Dave," I responded as I shook his hand. His grasp was tight and he had large, thick fingers with tattoos on each and every one of them.

"Yo' man, I think we might have gone to the same elementary school. You ever get taught by Mrs. Watkins?" Joe asked.

"Yeah, she taught fourth grade. My class was her last before she retired," I responded.

"Oh, so you're a lot younger than me and Eric," Joe said.

The third inmate lay silent on the top of my bunk. I stood to my feet and became eye level with him as he lay on his side with eyes wide open. "What's good? I'm Dave," I said. He didn't respond. His lips were shut tight but his eyes remained open and gazing right at me. He looked like he was a shell-shocked soldier on the beaches of Normandy. There were veins in the whites surrounding his corneas and the skin around his nose and forehead was wrinkled and dry. "He don't have no tongue," Eric said. "Some white motherfuckers ripped out at the last prison he was at. Just forget he's there," Joe immediately followed.

I turned and gazed around the vast space. It was loud. Every pocket had conversation rumbling. "It's like this before yard time every day," Eric said. The closest pocket to us was an Asian group and next to them were Pacific Islanders. Beyond them were some whites and running parallel to them were the Mexicans. We didn't fuck with either of those groups and one slip-up could have meant a solid beating or even death. But still, Eric said they were manageable. He seemed like a smart man. I continued to spin around and I saw Bloods and they were staring right back at me. These were the guys we had to look out for. In the Gym, it was a cold war that was always on the precipice of becoming hot.

"Think of the Gym as LA. There are parts where you have friends, and there are areas where you have enemies. Always know where you're at, and you'll be fine. If you enter enemy territory, you won't be fine. Got it?" Eric exclaimed.

"Are there more of us?" I said.

"Yeah, over there, over there, and... over there," Eric said as he pointed. "We only ever congregate in the yard. Too risky to be bouncing around in here," he followed.

The first group of allies was about six bunks away. One of our allies was a dude named Barney. I wouldn't get to know him better for a little while after that day. Those guys had the same tattoos that brothers from my neighborhood had. They were about ten years older than I was and you could tell they had all been in here for a long time. Their muscles were statue-esque and veins popped out from their coarse skin.

"You see that white guy over there?" Joe said as he pointed at a white man sitting alone on his bunk as his bearded white brethren conspired in a circle before him.

The white man was covered in tattoos that I had seen only in flashes of my memory. They were tattoos that a white boy shouldn't have. Brother tattoos... I didn't think something like that could be imprinted on white skin without steam sizzling from the penetrated point. "That dude is a Blood. His name's Jamie. He ain't allowed to be seen with the other bloods, so he's gotta roll with the white guys, even though they hate him for his affiliations," Joe followed. I had heard of white folk joining traditionally black gangs in California before but I had never seen it with my own eyes.

"What's his story?" I asked.

"He's from the hood, but he's gotta be the most hated motherfucker in here," Eric responded.

In my peripheral vision, I saw a silhouette that I had seen before. My gaze scanned left to a pocket of men no further than twelve bunks away and amongst them was a face I knew. I couldn't put my finger on it at first. The man had a big afro and thin eyebrows. His eyes slightly bulged out from their sockets and his nose was a little flat. My stare lingered on him as he played cards with a few other black men.

"Markus," I mumbled.

The last time I had seen Markus was at Auntie Cheryl's house when we were thirteen years old. We were the elders of that courtroom and Markus had seen his fair share of trials. There he was, right before me in a room full of some of the most dangerous criminals in California. There was nobody in the Gym that was innocent. I wanted to talk to him, to give him a hug, and ask him what happened in his life to bring him here. "I know that dude," I muttered.

"Who... Markus?" Eric said.

"Who's he with?" I asked.

"He ain't one of us, that's for sure, but he's probably in here for murder," Joe piped up.

I stared at my old friend with a linger but Markus was too preoccupied with his quartermates that he did not see me. I knew I had to say something to him or else the anticipation would eat me alive later that night. I was wary of my actions due to the severity of nightmares I was having. Every night my mind seemed to fluctuate between psychological suicide and perpetual repentance until I would jolt awake from my slumber covered in sweat and gasping for air. Seeing an old friend could counter that. I thought it could have brought me some solace in isolation and tamed the dreams that were corroding my brain.

I took one step toward Markus' bunk, then another, and another. Eric jumped up from his bed and grabbed me by the shoulders as I began my trek down the alley. "Dave," Eric yelled as he spun me around. He looked into my eyes with intensity and his fingers dug into my skin and muscles around my shoulder. "Where the hell are you going?" he asked. "I haven't seen Markus since I was a kid," I responded as I swatted his hands away. Eric pulled me back with an even greater force and I got mad. I could see heads turning in the Gym. Guards even gently held their hands over their holsters in case a fight was about to break out.

"Just cause you're my elder doesn't mean I won't set you straight. I'll risk the fucking DP," I said to Eric quietly.

Eric started laughing. I was mad, even madder than before. Eric leaned in closer and gently grasped my shoulder. "If you walk that way you'll get hit right in the spleen before you even know what's happening. You'll fall to your knees and drag yourself back here while you yell out for help and leave a trail of fresh blood behind you. You'll die, trust me, I've seen it. Joe and I both have," whispered Eric. "But, if you want to say hi to your little friend, go for it," he followed as he patted me on the shoulder and returned to his bunk.

I gazed down the aisle. Markus still hadn't seen me. He was so close I could practically smell him. Heads along the aisle were focused on me. Asians, blacks, and whites all within spitting distance of each other. All in arms reach of a black man with a history of killing. I returned to my bunk and sat on its edge. Eric smiled and nodded his head.

"You know why your bunk is open?" Joe asked.

"Why?"

"Because the last motherfucker, Jamal, walked down that aisle to buy heroin from the Asians and ended up catching a blade," Joe followed.

"Who did it?" I said as I looked at Eric.

"We never found out. Whoever did it has kept it pretty close," Eric responded.

Joe pushed himself up and he jumped down from the top bunk. He pointed at Eric and didn't blink. "You know damn well who did it," he yelled. Eric calmly stood to his feet. I stayed seated on the edge of the bunk, just gazing up at these two large black men coming within inches of each other's faces. "We don't know shit and we ain't gonna' do shit until we know shit," Eric said firmly.

"That motherfucker Jamie was holding a damn shiv that morning. The trail of blood led back to his pocket," Joe responded.

"It could have been any one of the other crackers," Eric said.

"Bullshit. He needed a way to prove himself and that's what he did," Joe said as he turned around and stared directly at Jamie.

Joe was a hot head and he was loyal. I could only imagine what he wanted to do to Jamie. His fists were clenched tightly and there was a rumble in his cheeks, but he composed himself enough to turn and climb onto his bunk. He lay on his back with wide eyes and heavy breaths as he gazed up at the silver ceiling constructed from aluminum.

I heard buzzing. I looked around but couldn't see anything. It was a loud noise, but not loud enough for any of the other bunks to hear it. Joe suddenly whipped a vibrating flip cell phone and pinned it to his ear. He scanned the room as he buried his face into his pillow. "Is that a phone?" I asked Eric.

"This Asian dude Tyler has a hookup. He can get you one for five hundred bucks," Eric responded. "I got one, too. How else are we supposed to talk to women?" he followed as he pulled out his flip phone.

Joe had a fat smile on his face as he baby talked to the chick on the other end of that line. I didn't know that was a thing yet. Nobody in Southern California had phones in incarceration when I was in my early twenties. To my knowledge, everybody just wrote letters or used the landlines when allowed. "What happens if you get caught?" I asked. Joe and Eric both turned to me. I could faintly hear the woman's voice through Joe's phone speaker. She was yelling and rambling on about something, but Joe didn't seem to care. He was staring at me instead.

"We ain't getting caught with these, y'understand? If that shit goes in your report, you ain't never getting parole," Joe muttered.

"That goes for any reprimandings. They're strict as hell, so don't shine any lights on us," Eric followed.

Joe resumed his call and lay back in his bunk. I stood to my feet to stretch my arms out wide. That place was hell from the start. It smelled like it, it looked like it, and it housed the kinds of people that belonged to be there, including me. My neck cracked as I forced it one way and then forced it the other way. I stood tall and put my arms behind my back and locked my fingers. Every vertebra of my spine cracked as I squeezed my arms together from behind. The popping sound echoed across the Gym. My chest felt thin and my stomach experienced the pain of a million thumbtacks rolling around within it. I was just about to call it a day when my gaze met that of Markus. He stood tall with a smirk on his face, staring right back at me. His boys were all arguing behind him and pushing each other with frustration. He just stood there silently, looking at me. He lifted his arm and extended the fingers on his hand out wide. I did the same. It felt good to see a familiar face again. He was a relic from a time when others had hope for me and my future. It was a time when I was the greatest lawyer Auntie Cheryl's courtroom had ever seen.

Caged Animals

A cold light rains down onto my skin. The moon projects cyan rays which illuminate the sky with a chilling blue. The stars are riddled across the galaxy and twinkle in the reflection of the glowing celestial body. I'm all alone. It's quiet. Only the noise of crickets chirping and birds squawking is heard but yet it is still faint enough to feel isolated. Before me is a wall of glass, and surrounding me are a few sparsely placed trees that climb fifteen feet into the air and rocky edges of small cliffs. There's nothing else.

"Hello?" I yell.

My words bounce between the walls and glass and echo until they fade off into the night. The wind howls from above before the leaves on the trees rustle with a delayed response. Their green skin reflects shades of blue from the moonlight and glows a cobalt color that pops like a flower in the desert. One by one the leaves adopt this shade until the entire tree sways in a motion of blue ecstasy. Trails of light swing from right to left and hang in suspension before fluttering to the ground like illuminated snowflakes. The light rains down onto me as I gaze upward at the falling glimmers of cobalt. Just as they are about to touch my skin, they disintegrate.

The wind falls to a lull and the tree stops swaying. The blue hue is sucked out of the vegetation and the leaves' natural green shade returns. The night grows darker once again with only the slight glimmer of the blue moon casting cold rays down onto me being present. "I've got to get out of here," I whisper to myself. I scan all directions, but where there is no glass, there is rock, and where there is no rock, there is glass. It's impossible to escape. Every exit is sealed. I saunter toward a tree and sit beneath it. I lean against the hardwood and its imperfect edges jab into my back. I don't care. No pain is worse than feeling constricted. I drop my head and look at the grass between my feet. My toes rub back and forth atop it. It tickles my soles. It's a feeling I haven't felt in a long time.

A thump at the glass echoes and sends a vibration along the ground. I feel it rumbling against my ass cheeks. I lift my head and my eyes shoot wide open. My heart stops and I choke up. My arms tremble as I plant my hands into the dirt and push myself to my feet slowly. My gaze remains direct and my breathing slows to a ticking beat. I step forward. The slight crunch of the grass and sticks beneath my step fills the silence that hangs in the air. My hand extends wide so that my fingers are fanned out and I plant my palm onto the cold glass. Her hand touches the glass on the other side. My eyes glisten with tears that rush from my heart like a landslide down a mountain's edge.

"Mom," I whisper.

My mother's arm is extended against the glass as she stares directly into my eyes. Her lips are sealed tight. She breathes slowly but harshly through her nose as if she is holding back her tears. "Mom, get me out of here," I say. She doesn't move an inch. Her hand stays on the glass and her lips remain tightened. The chilling divider becomes too much for me and I displace my palm from it and rub my fingers through my hair. My heart beats faster and my breaths are sharp and painful. I shake my head slowly as I look at her.

"Mom, please," I say with a growing hole in my heart.

Another thump rumbles against the glass and I whip my head to the right. My little brother William stands twenty feet from my mother on the other side of the glass and I run to him. "Will," I yell. He places his hand on the glass and spreads his fingers out wide. He stares at me with no emotion. The lid of his Dodgers cap shades his brown eyes. I feel like I'm looking at a silhouette. "William, listen to me, okay? You've got to listen to me," I start. It's getting harder to breathe. I lift my head to the blue moon and its cobalt rays cause discomfort in my eyes. The cold air desensitizes my cheeks until they are numb. Blotches of blue shift around my skin like bubbles in a lava lamp. It's so cold I feel like I can't move.

"Stay warm, Will," I say as my teeth chatter.

I exhale and a rush of steam populates the air before my mouth until it vanishes into the chilling sky. My arms tremble and I rub my hands over them, but it does no good. I close my eyes and bang my head against the glass. I'm as close as I can be to my brother. I can feel the palm of his hand touching my head through the thick pane of glass that separates us. I wish I could just talk to them, just to know what they really think of me.

I open my eyes and my feet have turned blue. My fingertips are frozen down to the bone and ice creeps along my hand until it reaches my wrist. I'm losing function everywhere. Steam exhales from my mouth and nose and it grows so chilling that I do not even shake. With every ounce of strength, I stand to my frozen feet and I turn my body to face my family. My neck creaks with the movement and the layer of ice atop my skin rushes up to my elbow. I exhale against the glass. It fogs up and distorts my view of the silhouette on the other side.

"William," I utter with a croaking voice.

The condensation on the glass is thick from my heavy breaths. I lift my arm before the ice rushes to my shoulder and paralyzes it in place. The steam on the glass slowly burns away and clarity strikes the transparent wall. On the other side is no man; it is a woman. I squint my eyes. I gasp. The cold air dries my throat and I barely congest enough oxygen to survive for one last breath. Standing on the other side of the glass is Auntie Cheryl. She looks exactly as she did when I was a boy. Her light, floral overthrow, and hunched back are clear as day. The tears on my cheeks freeze to droplets of ice and crack off my skin and smash atop the frozen ground at my feet.

"Auntie Cheryl," I mumble through the chatter of my teeth.

My mother, William, and Auntie Cheryl all stand side by side, staring at me with dead eyes and sealed lips. They watch as the ice creeps along my body until everything but my neck and head are frozen. I am held in place, locked away for eternity, forced to view the world through a pane of glass. The cold is my environment and I may never feel the embrace of warmth again. My vision fades and the shimmering silhouettes of my loved ones glimmer as they fade into total, utter blackness. The night is dark and the chill is unforgiving. The flame that burns within me dwindles and sways from side to side, ready to extinguish at any given moment. I could really die here.

The First Domino

My bones shook in the middle of the night. My sheets were covered in sweat. I had awoken yet again with sharpness in my lungs. It was a struggle to inhale. It felt like nails were shredding my esophagus with every inhale. My nightmares had adjusted to the Gym. They were more intense. I felt the loneliness of them creep into reality. The Gym was like the jungle, and I couldn't escape the feeling of terror even in my slumber. The wild animal within me barked and growled, looking to be set free.

The Gym was thinning out as people flooded to the exit to see their loved ones. It was around Christmas, so it was the most popular time for visitors to come. I had the rest of my life to serve. That Christmas visitation day could have marked my ten-year milestone for all I knew. It did not matter to me. That day could have just been any old day like the ones that preceded it. They all seemed to have morphed into a single feeling that balanced my nostalgia and fear.

"I can't wait to see this woman," Joe said with a smile on his face.

"My chick should be here any minute," Eric added.

"Where's your bitches at, Dave?" Joe asked.

"Shut the fuck up," I responded.

"Don't worry, Dave. My girl's got a sister. I'll set you up," Eric said before he and Joe laughed uncontrollably.

A phone buzzed and Joe slipped it out of his pocket. He scanned around for the eyes of guards but the coast was clear. The buttons clicked as his fingers rapidly slammed atop them. "All right, boys, she's here. Time to see if she's a catfish or not," Joe said as he slipped the phone under his pillow. He stretched his arms high into the air, then he closed his hand to a fist and bumped Eric, then he bumped me. "Before I go I got some news for y'all," he followed. Eric and I looked at him. He festered at the moment, allowing the anticipation to linger until one of us exploded with impatience.

"Well... What the fuck is it?" Eric exclaimed.

"I made a plan," he said.

"And?"

"I'm gonna get my GED. Gonna really keep my head down, man. I want to get out of here. I'm talking about parole, man," Joe followed.

"Yeah right," Eric said with a chuckle.

"Seriously, man. I'm up for parole next year and I ain't never got nothing on my record. I think I can keep my head down long enough to be approved, man. I'm serious, I mean it."

The air was quiet. Joe nodded to us and turned his back. "Wish me luck," he said. Eric and I were silent. We didn't see it coming, so we didn't know what to say. Joe had a history of being violent. At night he would tell Eric and me stories from the streets. Like me, Joe was a fighter. He was in juvie more than five times and he always found the blunt end of a deadly object clenched in his steady hand. He had bruises and scars from bloody battles. His eyes had a look that made you wonder what was behind them. He was a killer, after all. All three of us were, and we knew that we were bad guys. Joe admitting he wanted something more for himself came at an opportune time. I had been having deadlier nightmares about incarceration and I knew that my conscience was trying to speak to me. I wanted to talk back, but I didn't see the point. I was a murderer in the eyes of the law and the law is unforgiving for a gangster who dedicated his life to a cause that opposed society's rules.

"Good for him," Eric mumbled.

"Yeah..."

"You ever thought about getting your degree in here?"

"You know, you ain't the first guy to ask me that... Don't see much of a point, really," I responded.

"Well, you should. I did, before I met Joe," Eric said. "Also... You've never gotten in trouble in here either, Dave. What's stopping you from trying to get parole?" Eric followed.

"You really asking me that? You know my story. I got fifteen to life, man. You know how the system works. I'm never getting out of here."

"All I'm saying is... You keep to yourself, man. You're smart. You only sell drugs when you need money, and you only do drugs when the coast is clear. You don't start fights. You don't raise your voice. You may not express it, but you got a plan too, motherfucker," Eric said as he slipped his phone under his pillow.

Eric was well-respected within these walls. People knew him as a family man without a family. He had a chick on the outside, and she was loyal. I wanted Eric to set me up with her sister, but she lived hundreds of miles away. He was seen as a level-headed guy who wouldn't unnecessarily engage in anything unless the reasoning was rooted in loyalty. That was his bag. He dapped me up and joined the line of people waiting to be admitted into the visitation room. I sat on my bunk all alone, watching as the hordes of people walked by.

"Dave," a whisper echoed.

I turned my head and Markus was standing in the aisle by my pocket. He scanned his surroundings and then took a couple steps toward me. "Yo man," I said. Markus exhaled and leaned against my bunk. His crew had all left the Gym and were currently in the visitation room, so it was just us. We didn't get many moments alone. Although he rolled with some black guys, too, it was taboo for us to communicate like that in the Gym. You could only have conversations in certain areas of the prison, like during work shifts, or during softball games when the weather was good. I worked in the kitchen and Markus didn't work at all. I'd usually give him a nod when I slapped mashed potatoes onto his tray. He'd sometimes wave his dry hand at me from across the Gym every once in a while when the coast was clear.

"Who you got seeing you today?" he said.

"My ma, and Will. How about you?"

"My daddy, man. His first time coming to see me," Markus responded with a smile.

"Tell him I said what's good."

Markus hunkered down by my bed. He scanned the room once more. His lips were sealed and I could see that his mind was running a million miles an hour. "You all right?" I asked. He lowered his head and looked at the legs of his orange overalls and black shoes. He exhaled through his nostrils. "Nah man, I ain't," he said. The chatter of inmates had dwindled to a near lull. There were only a handful of inmates left over. They were the ones who had no visitors. They had no loved ones who cared enough to come and see them before the holiday came and went. It wasn't even a thought in their mind that Markus and I were breaking Gym rules and talking with each other. At that time, I couldn't fathom what that really felt like.

"Do you ever worry about what your ma' thinks of you?"

"Sure, man," I responded.

"I mean what she really thinks of you. The stuff that she would never say out loud. You know, I'm talking about the subconscious," Markus said to me without blinking.

"Why are you asking me this?"

"Because you're the only one I can ask."

I didn't know what to say to Markus, and he knew that. I patted him on the shoulder and we both rose to our feet. I could feel the weight of guilt sitting on his conscience. He had a look in his eye that wanted to be seen, one that expressed his call for help. I knew and I still did not know what to say. All I could do was walk alongside somebody I once considered a great friend. We approached the guards standing by the door that led out of the Gym. I let Markus go before me. All the lined up inmates were quiet. A new guard was calling out names. He was Officer Jacob. His voice would boom and holler with every incarcerated man approved for visitation.

"Spivey, you're up," Jacob yelled.

I was put in handcuffs and led to the visitation room. It was sealed off by a large metallic door. I stood by it and gazed at the red light shining in a caged-off bulb above the frame. Its magenta rays cast soft rays onto the wall surrounding it. A buzz rang through the air and the light flashed green. The door unlocked and the guard next to me placed his giant hand on the metal and pushed it open. The chatter of inmates and their loved ones reverberated through the air. The loud sounds of crying, yelling, laughing, sniffling, and sneezing hung in suspension as I walked through the door and was met with a blinding bright white light that illuminated the entire space. The visitation room was much bigger than anywhere else I had been incarcerated. It was able to fit about a hundred and fifty inmates, with two visitors per jailbird. We would sit at these desks that reminded me of elementary school. You would chill on one side, and your visitor or visitors would go on the other side. Guards would line the perimeter and watch the floor from vantage points. They held batons in their hands but rarely was it ever threatening. They knew that most of us were looking forward to visitation day and that to screw it up for one person meant screwing it up for everyone. If someone caused a big scene and had everyone thrown out, then that dude would be catching a shiv later that night. Every decision you made had to be rooted in respect.

My mom and William were sitting at a table at the far end of the room. I walked by a dozen dudes that would have loved to have me dead, but they didn't even glance at me. They were all wrapped up in the conversations they were having. Some of us waited months and years to unleash the words to those who visited. We carefully curated our speech for that very moment. Each night, looking up at the aluminum ceiling and metal pipes that ran from one end to the other, our minds would be consumed by the stories we wanted to tell those on the outside. It was moments like these that motivated a lot of us to keep hanging on, as we knew that when one passed, another would eventually come.

"Hi, mom. Hi Will," I said as I sat opposite my family.

"Man, you're looking skinny as hell," Will exclaimed.

"I work out every day, motherfucker," I responded with a chuckle.

Will and I laughed together a lot. We were really close. I missed him every minute that I wasn't talking to him. He showed up to the visitation wearing baggy clothes and a Dodgers cap. It was the uniform I used to wear when I was his age. I could tell my mom hated it, but she knew that her words would just fly off into dark space. "You got a girl?" I asked my brother. He puckered his lips and leaned back. "I got girls, bro. Plural," he said with a smile. My mom shook her head but I could see a little smile. She wanted us to be gentlemen but she knew better than to ask a young man to act in such a way.

"How about you, momma? How are you doing?" I asked.

"I'm good, baby," she responded quietly.

"Yo' Dave, I have got to tell you something crazy," Will said as he leaned over the desk.

"Hey!" A yell echoed from Officer Jacob across the hall. He slammed his baton against the metal perimeter, then he pointed the stick right at my brother. Heads of inmates and families were all directed at us. I lifted both my tied hands and nodded my head to apologize. "Sit back down, Will. You ain't allowed to do that in here," I said. Chatter resumed and the guard slipped his baton back in his holster. My mom gently dragged Will back into his seat and patted him on the thigh.

"My bad, Dave. I didn't mean to get you in trouble," Will said. "I was just gonna' say... You remember Lil' Mike?" he followed.

"Lil' Mike from the neighborhood?"

"Yeah."

"What about him?"

"They found him dead last night... Couple bullet holes in his head," William said as my mother closed her eyes and shook her head.

"You're kidding. He wasn't even about that life," I responded.

"Must have pissed off the wrong dude or something," Will said with a shrug of his shoulders.

Lil' Mike was a bad kid, but he did turn his life around when we were teenagers. His parents were both drug addicts and he never had a light guiding him through life. He walked alone in darkness and fought for himself. I think that's why he was such a misbehaved kid. But, when I first joined the gang, I distinctly remember Lil' Mike stepping away from us. He stayed at home more often playing video games. I thought he had just become a loser, but the older I grew, the more I realized that he was restricting himself from trouble. He got a job as a mailman, or a garbage man, or something like that. To have heard that he died a murderous death surprised me, and even made me a little sad. I don't know why it happened, but I know he didn't deserve it.

"That's not all, honey," my mom said.

"You good, momma'?" I asked.

"Auntie Cheryl passed away last week. She died of old age," she followed with a choke in her words.

"Auntie Cheryl?"

"I got to see her at the hospital before she went... She told me to tell you that she still has faith in you, even after what you did."

After a certain point in my life, Auntie Cheryl really only existed in my dreams. I hadn't actually seen her in years, since I was a boy. She only knew me for a short period of my life but my mom must have given her updates whenever she could. "She always thought so highly of you, David," my mom said to me. Her kindness was potent. It was something you could sense. From her gaze to her touch, to her words, she was somebody who I knew I would miss.

"I can't believe it," I said.

"You never think about that sort of thing, do you, baby?"

"What do you mean, mom?"

"How time passes you by outside. How people get old and die after a life spent living. You never think about that, do you?"

She was right. I rarely thought about that. In prison, your mind had to be present within the walls that confined you at all times. You had to stay aggressive or be a victim. If you started to think about life outside, you were fucked. You became unconsolable, knowing that nothing you could do would change the fact that you were incarcerated. It made you weak and weakness was not tolerated. The only time you were allowed to show emotion like that was when a loved one died.

"Can I ask you something, mom?"

"Sure, baby," she responded.

"What do you think of me? Like really think of me..."

"You and William are the loves of my life. Without you both, I don't exist. Sometimes I wish more for myself, and sometimes I accept what I have. The reality is, David, you're in here paying for your sins, and your brother is out there following in your footsteps... Nothing I say, think, or do will change that reality."

That hour felt like five minutes. Seeing my mom and brother was something I had been waiting for, and when they were asked to leave when the time limit approached, I wanted to go with them. The last thing I wanted to do was return to the Gym, where I would sleep with one eye open and carefully curate my speech so I didn't initiate a fight. It was exhausting. I was aging like a pint of spoiled milk. Time was a resource, and I was poor. I wanted them to stay with me and never leave. I was a young boy again who just wanted to be embraced by his loved ones.

I returned to my bunk to find Joe and Eric in theirs, lying on their backs and just gazing upwards. The entire Gym was quiet. You could hear the creaking of metal from the poorly constructed beds. The sound of the wind blowing outside caused a gentle but howling echo that reverberated around the space. "Psst. Dave, she wasn't a catfish," Joe whispered to me. I tried not to laugh. I sat on my bunk and stared down at the concrete floor. My breathing was slow but my heart beat fast. I thought about my mom and brother hopping into a car and driving to the motel they were staying at for the night. They had never been this far up north. It was their first time seeing all of the evergreen trees and rocky landscapes that spanned for miles. It wasn't the inner city where car horns and yelling consumed the air.

A pair of black shoes stepped into my gaze and I lifted my head with my fists clenched. It was Tyler, and he had his hands in his pockets. "I heard you were in the market," he mumbled to me. Eric and Joe rolled over in their bunks and looked at me. I met their contact and with wide eyes, I telepathically asked them if I should strike before being struck. "It's all good, Dave. I told him you didn't have a cell phone and you had the money to get one," Eric whispered. Tyler crouched down and removed a flip phone from one of his pockets. He presented it to me in his palm. The tips of his fingers were perspiring and there were Japanese symbols tattooed on his forearm. I slowly grabbed the phone and inspected it. I flipped it open and all of the keys lit up in a bright white light. The screen had a solid blue background with white numbers glowing on it that showed the time.

"You can call, text, and even use the internet," Tyler whispered.

"How much?" I asked.

"Six hundred."

"I heard you sell 'em for five hundred," I responded.

"That's for the older models. This one's brand new, see?"

Tyler grabbed the phone back and pointed to its outer shell. He rubbed his fingers along the metallic casing and then pulled out an antenna. He held the phone to his ear and mimicked being called. I could smell a scam artist from a mile away, and I wasn't an easy target. "Yo' Tyler," Eric whispered from his bunk. " Keep true to your word, you scumbag," he followed.

"All right, five hundred," Tyler said reluctantly.

The phone felt heavy in my hands. I pulled out five, one hundred dollar bills from beneath my pillow and handed them to Tyler. It was all I had. He tip-toed away carefully and quietly. I flipped the device open and the keyboard lit up. The artificial illumination cast rays on my face and a glow in my eyes. The lights of the Gym suddenly faded and a guard yelled, "Lights out!". I quickly closed my phone and the Gym was cast in darkness until the sun was to rise once again.

"I hope that makes things a little less lonely for you, brother," Eric whispered from within the blackness.

"How about you give me your girl's sister's number now?" I asked.

"Her name is Nadine, you horny motherfucker," Eric responded with a chuckle.

A smile struck my face as I lay back in my bunk. The phone sat on my chest and I closed my eyes with my hands resting atop the device. The sound of the wind and creaking bunks seemed to fade away into the night, and peace washed over me for the first time in a long time. I could see those little blotches of fuzzy light dancing around in the blackness of my inner eye socket. It was the most peaceful moment I would have had in that prison. I never could have anticipated the way life turned after that winter night.

Back in Business

I felt a jagged pit in my stomach. It was painful. The sharp edges jabbed into my guts and heart and I struggled to focus on anything other than the negative thoughts the issue brought with it. It was one of those feelings I had when something bad was going to happen. Most days, I was just prepared for an altercation, but there were some days, every so often, that I would genuinely feel like I was in danger. I had been experiencing fewer nightmares, but I knew that one was coming. The dread was building from deep inside me and bubbling to the surface of my psyche. I scanned the Gym and looked at all the different types of faces before me. Every single one of them expressed their ability to murder through their gaze alone. There was nothing behind the eyes. I thought about which one of them wanted it most. Who would benefit the greatest from my demise? I didn't know. The whispers in the Gym were quiet and only came around once. It meant that the "truth" was rarely what it seemed. It changed with every ear it entered and mouth it exited. For all I knew, I could have had a great enemy in that prison.

The air was cool that spring day. Everybody was beaming to go out to the yard. It had been raining torrentially for the last month or so. The constant sound of raindrops whacking against the aluminum roof rang through the space. I feared that the rain would never end. It was a consistent reminder that a world did exist outside those walls. No amount of TV, radio, or cell phone usage could have had the same effect on me. It was always the weather that manipulated my emotions.

I played a game of 'Snake' on my phone as I lay back in my bunk. Eric was texting his girl. Joe read through a book. I set my device down and stood to my feet. I approached the side of Joe's bunk and nudged his shoulder. "What're you reading?" I asked. Joe sighed and carefully put the book down flat. He didn't look happy. "It's my GED study book, asshole... I can get parole easier if I pass," he responded. I ripped the book from him and scanned through it quick enough to realize that he was in the mathematics section. He slapped me in the face and ripped the book out of my hands. Eric and I couldn't contain our laughter.

"Can't get shit done around here," Joe mumbled as he re-opened the book.

"We're just playing, man," I said.

Eric shut his flip phone and slid it into one of his boots under the bunk. He stood to his feet and stretched his arms out wide. "You got any weed, Dave?" Eric asked. "Nah," I responded. I had been craving marijuana for weeks, maybe even months. I had spent all my money on my phone and my phone plan. I tried hard not to do drugs because in the Gym it was difficult to get away with it. There simply wasn't a reason to be sparking up inside. Because of the bad weather, we hadn't had a good yard day, so you couldn't smoke outside either without the joint getting wet. Today was a nice day, and Eric and I wanted to embrace it.

"I got an idea," I said.

I snatched my phone and shoved it into my pocket. I looked to the nearest group of my allies and their bunks were within spitting distance. I carefully walked down the aisle, scanning my vision with every step to see if anyone I was passing was holding a shiv. My steps were quiet and calculated and I strayed away from arm's reach every chance I got. I had my eyes on a dude named Barney. Motherfuckers called him that because he kind of looked like the kid's TV show dinosaur. He was big and burly and had a fat face. He even walked like Barney.

"Yo' Barney," I called out.

Barney turned, and so did his three bunkmates. We were all cool. They knew we all had the same loyalties and beliefs. I dabbed them all up, and then removed my cell phone from my pocket and presented it to him. "I been hearing you're looking for a phone," I said. "I'll rent you mine for the whole day in exchange for two spliffs," I followed. Barney puckered his lips and nodded his head. He was staring down at the flip phone in my hands. I knew what was on his mind. He had a baby momma' and two kids. He loved his children and every phone call he got he made it to them. They were his reason for staying positive and he was just waiting for the day that he could get released so he could go and see them.

"All right, deal," Barney said.

I handed the phone over and he rolled me up two spliffs on the spot. I returned to my bunk with a little bag and dangled it in front of Eric. A fat smile struck his face. "You sure you don't want to join?" I asked Joe. "I'm positive," he responded. Joe sighed, closed his GED book, and then sat on the edge of his bunk with his legs hanging over the edge. He rubbed his temples with his fingers.

"This shit is so fucking hard, man," he mumbled.

Joe took a deep breath and lifted his head. His gaze immediately caught something in the distance and he lifted his finger to point. "Yo' look," he said. Eric and I turned our heads and looked to the pocket of white folk several bunks away. Three large, bearded dudes were surrounding Jamie and they looked mad. One of them pushed Jamie and he fell backward and onto his ass in the middle of the aisle. "I'll fucking kill you for that, motherfucker," Jamie yelled as he pushed himself back up and charged at all three men. He stood no chance against all of them and he got a royal beating for about fifteen seconds before a gang of guards rushed over and broke it all up.

"If I see you assholes fighting one more time it's going on your record," the guard screamed. Jamie's face was covered in blood. He shook as he pushed himself to his feet and stumbled onto his bunk. He sighed and closed his eyes as he pinched the bridge of his nose to stop the blood from rushing out. "Motherfucker deserves worse," Joe said. I looked at the clock on the wall of the Gym and it was almost noon. I was dying to get outside and smell the fresh spring air. That feeling of doom still lingered in my mind.

A loud buzz rang through the Gym. Several guards began marching toward the exit door to the yard. "All right, line up," a guard yelled out. Everybody migrated slowly and carefully to the door. Those closest to the exit went out first, guys in the middle, like me, went next, and then dudes at the back of the Gym spilled out last. The air was chilling but the sky was clear and the sun hung bright in suspension. The trees were still as green as I had last remembered and the grass outside the gates was tall and unkempt.

"Follow me," Eric said.

Joe held his book and studied as he walked alongside me. Eric led the way through a sea of inmates of all kinds of races and gangs. It was the exact same as before. There were Asians, whites, blacks of various gang backgrounds, and Native Americans who stayed out of the way and protected their own. I even saw Markus among his group of killers. They walked in a unit across the grassy plains, puffing out their chests. Markus nodded to me and I nodded back. Segregation was a constant, but I was beginning to see that the situation in that institution, compared to Southern California, was more covert. Nobody was screaming and yelling in the yard. People plotted instead, just waiting for the right moment to strike.

"Over here," Eric exclaimed as he pointed at an empty bench.

We sat down and a splinter immediately jabbed into my butt. I stood up and pulled it out slowly. It stung like a motherfucker, but I sat back down carefully and removed the two spliffs from the little bag in my pocket. Joe continued to read through his GED book. A spark exploded from the tip of my lighter and burnt the tips of the two spliffs at once. I handed one to Eric, and we both leaned back and took it all in.

"You been having nightmares?" Eric asked.

"Nah, I'm cool," I responded.

"I hear you shifting around at night and mumbling and shit."

"I'm asleep, motherfucker. How am I supposed to know I'm moving around and shit?"

Eric shrugged his shoulders and took a long drag of the spliff. My dreams were visceral and the terror that stemmed from them was pungent. It was the same feeling I had been having all day. The premonition of an unfortunate event pumped through my mind. I scanned the yard through the smoke that was rising from the joint that burned in my right hand. Markus stood among his crew. His fellow gangsters lifted weights while he smoked a cigarillo and spotted them. His lips were wrapped tightly around the butt and veins popped out from his biceps as he grabbed hold of the weight bar and helped his gang member finish his set.

From the corner of my eye, I spotted something. I shifted my gaze and squinted my eyes to try to get a good look. Through the gaps in the bodies of inmates, I saw Jamie shifting through crowds of various criminals all by his lonesome. He wore a wife beater and his Blood tattoos were on display for the world to see. He sauntered with his hands in his pockets. Heads turned as he walked by. Growling noises echoed along with the clicking sound of clenching jaws. Fists were tightened and blades were grabbed from inside the orange overall pockets of murderers. That man was a lone buffalo in the center of a herd of hungry lions.

"Jamie's got a death wish," Eric muttered.

Joe's eyes lifted from his GED book. They moved slowly left, watching the path Jamie was on several hundred yards before us. Warm air exhaled from Joe's nostrils and onto the cream-colored pages of the book. The air rushed down as if he were a bull ready to charge a matador. He carefully set the book down on the bench and stood to his feet. "What're you thinking, Joe?" Eric asked. Joe didn't respond at first. He probably didn't even hear Eric. His mind was living in the hypothetical world where he held a Glock 45 that was pressed against Jamie's head.

"I promised Jamal that I'd kill whoever murdered him. I promised him that during his dying breath..." Joe muttered.

Eric stood to his feet and held the spliff in his mouth as he placed both his hands on Joe's shoulders. Joe shimmied Eric off and took a step forward. "Joe, don't be stupid," Eric exclaimed. I sat quietly on the bench. The yard was silent, like we were in the eye of the storm. Jamie had been parting the trail clear before him. He walked right up to the gang of Bloods and stood tall. It was inaudible from where I was sitting, but I could tell he was pleading for his life. He wanted to be with the men he was loyal to, but the looks on their faces showed that it wasn't a possibility. Jamie flayed his arms about and his yells were faint from the distance at which I sat. "I'm one of you!" he yelled and yelled. A large black man stood tall before Jamie and pushed him back. Jamie had a look of disbelief on his face. His shoulders had dropped low and his neck was slightly bent to the side. He kneeled before his gang members for just a moment, until the wind blew and the men turned their backs to him. Jamie was paralyzed in place as hundreds of us inmates gazed at him, all by himself.

Joe reached into his pocket and pulled out a knife. He concealed it with his hand and began walking toward Jamie. "Joe!" Eric bellowed. Joe wasn't turning around. He wasn't even listening to the sounds of the yard. His vision was tunneled and focused on one thing only. His steps turned to stomps and the grass flattened with every pound against it. Inmates turned and stepped back to clear the way for Joe.

"Motherfucking idiot... I can't let him do this," Eric exclaimed before tossing his spliff and jumping to his feet.

Eric sprinted in Joe's direction. I tossed my spliff and stood on the bench to get a good look. I quickly realized I was alone, so every other moment I would scan my surroundings to make sure nobody was creeping up on me. All eyes were on Joe. He was making ground and Jamie was no more than fifty yards from him. "Joe!" Eric yelled out as he ran at him from behind. Joe turned and Eric immediately tackled him to the ground. I jumped off the bench. My knees clicked as I landed on the grass and I almost fell. The lack of exercise had made me weaker. I began jogging to the action. Joe and Eric rolled in the grass. Eric tried to pin Joe down but Joe was strong and pushed back in an attempt to roll Eric off him so he could get back to his feet. The veins in their necks popped out and displayed red and blue crooked lines that ran along their dry skin. Their muscles bulged and sweat poured down their foreheads.

"Get the fuck off me, Eric," Joe yelled.

"You're gonna' ruin your life, man," Eric responded.

Eric flipped Joe over and pulled his left arm behind his back. Joe screamed out in pain and kicked like a bucking donkey. "The guards are gonna' come and if you ain't chill, then we're both getting written up," Eric said calmly. Joe squirmed beneath Eric's weight but as I approached and stood over my friends, I could see tears swell in Joe's eyes. He stopped flaying his legs about and he lay calmly, faced down in the grass.

"Get the fuck off me," Joe said quietly.

Eric pushed himself off Joe and stood tall. He wiped the grass off his orange jumpsuit. Joe took a deep breath and sat on the ground. He scanned around him, looking into the eyes of the inmates that had surrounded the conflict. Then, he looked at Jamie, who stared right back at him. "What the fuck are you looking at?" Joe yelled. Jamie turned his back and walked away from the area. Joe shook his head. I extended my arm and helped him up. All three of us walked back to the bench together, parting the sea of curious criminals that had gathered. Not a word was spoken.

We were lucky the guards didn't rush over. If that happened, Eric and Joe would have both gotten a point on their record. They would have been sent to the box. I would have been left all alone, probably for weeks. The Gym was cold enough as it was. That isolation would have frozen me to death. That pit in my stomach had only grown stronger as the day went on. The feeling of impending doom loomed over my head like a thunderous rain cloud and followed me in every direction.

The skies above the yard soon turned gray with shadowy clouds rolling over the jailhouse. Droplets of rain sprinkled down onto us all. I perched my neck backward and gazed up at the fluttering raindrops falling from the heavens. I took a deep breath and closed my eyes. I could feel the watery sensation clean my face of sweat and dirt. The smell of spring lingered in my nostrils. It reminded me of Auntie Cheryl's backyard. She maintained it and treated each blade of grass like it was one of her children. The world was quiet once more until a booming pound of thunder rattled the sky. My eyes jolted open and a flash of lightning illuminated from within the ominous gray clouds.

"Everybody line up!" Officer Jacob yelled through a megaphone as he stood upright with a stern look on his face.

The rain started to come down harder. Each droplet lashed against the heads of every man who stood in a queue by the door, waiting to be allowed inside by the guards who patrolled the line with batons. I stood behind Joe, who was behind Eric. Joe had his GED book stuffed into his orange overalls so it would stay dry. Inmates grew rowdy as the storm intensified above. "Stay in your place until you are called," the guard yelled through his megaphone. I turned and looked to the back of the line. About a hundred people were waiting in a row behind me. I could see Markus' arm a dozen steps back. He was standing still with his hands down by his hips.

"Next ten," the guard yelled.

Eric, Joe, and I walked back into the Gym like a pack of wet dogs and went right for our bunks. Water dripped through cracks in the aluminum ceiling and ran down the walls. The sound of wet shoes hitting the Gym floor filled the air. The coils of beds squeaked when inmates jumped into their cots. I sat on the edge of mine and watched as Joe and Eric pulled out their cell phones and checked their messages. "Oh, come on," Joe sighed. "Motherfucker," he yelled as he smashed his phone against the floor. It shattered into dozens of pieces which scattered across the Gym in an instant. Joe put his head in his hands.

"Yo, yo, you good?" Eric asked.

"That bitch dumped me for some punk ass Mexican dude," Joe muttered. "Some fucking day today has been," he followed as he laid back in his bed and covered his eyes with his hands. Eric looked at me and nodded. I returned the gesture, and Eric lay down in his bed and played on his phone. All of the inmates had entered the Gym and the guards slammed the door shut. The noise echoed throughout the space. "All right everyone, lights out in thirty minutes," a guard yelled. The tapping of raindrops became a constant, but the heavy breathing of Joe was most apparent.

"Yo' Dave," a voice bellowed.

I turned and Barney stood tall behind me. He looked around for a moment, then he stuck his hand in his orange pocket and removed my cell phone. "Thank you, my baby momma' been giving me a lot of shit recently and this made her happy. Appreciate you," he said. The phone was warm and the battery had been nearly drained to the bottom. I nodded to Barney and he turned and stomped back to his pocket of allies.

The phone powered on and lights illuminated around the perimeter of the buttons. The screen glowed a bright blue. I pulled up my mother's contact number and I typed out a message while whispering the words along to myself; "I miss you, momma'. I'm gonna give you a call in the morning. The weather was finally good enough today for us to go outside for a few hours. Talk to you tomorrow. Love, Dave."

The lights of the Gym soon faded into darkness and all that remained of the day was that gut feeling. That horrendous, horrifying sensation of doom lingered over my bunk and I knew it would haunt my dreams just as it had haunted my awakened consciousness. Whatever was infecting my dreams had crept its way into reality, and I fell asleep that night knowing that when I awoke my life would no longer be the same. I just couldn't have imagined how pivotal a moment in my life it would be.

A Proustian Premonition

There is a familiar smell that hangs in the air. The California heat rolls in through the opened kitchen windows and makes its way around the home. I arise from my bed as the sun emerges in the sky and its ember rays pierce through the glass of my window. My eyes jolt wide open and I look outside. There is a hazy orange that hangs in the air and the streets are quiet and empty. The sun burns intensely bright and high outside the glowing, cloudless atmosphere. I look at the calendar on my wall. It's the morning of my court date. Veins are popping out in my stinging eyes and my arms shake as I open my closet and see my navy suit hanging neatly from a lone hanger.

My face frowns and wrinkles pop from my forehead. I stand before the mirror in my room and look at myself. A thump echoes from the first floor. "Mom?" I yell. A plate smashes. A chair screeches. My breathing slows to a near lull and I tip-toe toward my ajar bedroom door. It squeaks as I lightly swing it open and put one leg out into the second-floor hallway. The floorboards creak. A warm breeze flows along the surface of the ground and circumnavigates my ankles.

"Will?" I yell.

A thump reverberates. The house and walls shake. Dust sprinkles from the ceiling and down onto my head. I stand at the top of the staircase looking down. There are framed pictures along the wall of my mother, William, and myself. The hallway at the bottom has a red hue to it. Strands of shimmering blotches of heat dance in the atmosphere. I walk toward it. Sweat bullets form on my forehead and roll down to my chin. Another thump echoes from the kitchen. Pots and pans clank. "Who the fuck is it?" I yell as I creep down the last step of the staircase.

The carpet floor in the hallway is a light brown color yet completely spotless. The strands of the wool stick between my toes as I gently step along the banks of the wall. There is an opened door ten feet ahead and on the right. A warm ember glow of light shines through the opening and casts a shadow of illumination onto the wall opposite it. I can see particles of dust floating in the wall of sun rays. My heart beats faster. It thumps against the inside of my chest. The sounds of heavy breathing rumble from the kitchen the closer I get. I stand at the doorway's edge and I inhale slowly.

The walls rattle once more as I jump into the light that is cast through the doorway and into the hallway. It burns my eyes and I shield them with my forearm and turn my head to the side. "Motherfucker," I mutter. My vision is blurred but through the opened doorway the outlines of appliances and objects in the kitchen are visible. In the corner of my eye, I see the hazy and blurred outline of a black silhouette sitting in a chair at the top of the table. It's where my mother sits when we have a family dinner. I whip my head toward the figure and before I can get the words out it completely vanishes into thin air. My eyes adjust to the light and my full sight comes back. The warm ember rays saunter through the opened windows and illuminate the white and brown kitchen in a maroon hue. There isn't anybody in here, but the seat at the top of the table is pulled out and freezing to touch.

The walls rattle in place and dust falls from the ceiling once more. It comes down thick, like snowflakes fluttering from gray clouds at the beginning of a winter storm. Empty shampoo bottles fall and clatter against the base of the bathtub in the first-floor bathroom. The muttered echo of the creature is loud. Whatever it is, it's rattling around the bathroom and knocking everything over. I pick up a knife from the kitchen and tiptoe toward the room. My nostrils flare out wide and my eyes are focused ahead. The palms of my hand perspire as they wrap around the base of the sharpened kitchen knife which glistens in the red light.

"Show me who you are," I yell out to the creature.

The bathroom door cracks in half when I put my foot through it. The knob flies across the bathroom and smashes against the white tile wall on the other side. I break through the crushed wood and grasp the knife with all my might. Splinters are riddled across the floor and I navigate them expertly with a careful step. I scan my surroundings but the room is small. There's nowhere to hide. As I shift my gaze slowly around the space, I catch my reflection in the mirror and the knife slips from my hand and clanks against the tiled floor. My hair is freshly cut and there's a gold chain around my thin and muscled neck. My shoulders are big and broad and I don't have a shred of facial hair. My wet fingertips rub along my clear and clean skin. Youth exerts itself from my pores. Immaturity swarms my presence like flies on shit. I'm just a boy.

Television static rings through the air and I place my hands over my ears. The pitch grows and grows until it pierces my eardrums. I fall to my knees and close my stinging eyes. My heart thumps like a pounding drum. My esophagus thins and the energy to pull each breath greatens. The world shakes and I feel my brain rattling from side to side. Then, it all stops. There is complete silence. My arms shake as I push myself to my feet and step out of the kitchen and into the hallway.

The red hue darkens and I turn to my right to gaze at the front door. Its white paint is tarnished by the red light and the golden doorknob more-so resembles bronze. It vibrates in the frame. I can see the latches rattle and move ever so slightly. The carpet frizzes up and the wool stands tall. I rub my feet over it carefully and feel the tickling sensation against my soles. Hairs on my body perch up and rub against the insides of my clothes. A chilling stroke shoots up my spine and I stop, paralyzed in place right as my hand is about to touch the door handle. My fingertips shake as I use all my force to grab the knob. My sweat glistens in the red light. The fingertips rub ever so gently against the golden handle. It's cool, cold like the inside of a freezer. A whistling wind echoes from outside and the door shakes harshly in the frame. I take a step back and without warning the door is ripped from its latches and sucked into the glowing red and orange sky above. I stand in place gazing through the frame as blotches of heat and light shimmer in the doorway. I walk into the frame and I lift my gaze. The light burns my eyes but I squint and look at the shimmering red sun in the apocalyptic sky. Flames break through the atmosphere and spray fire across the painted background above Inglewood. Embers fall from great heights and set fire to the roofs of surrounding homes. The maroon reflection in my wide eyes glistens as I stand paralyzed looking at the world end before me.

"David," a soft voice echoes. "David, baby," the voice follows.

The hairs on my neck are high and stretched as straight as an arrow. They might snap in half at any moment. The bones in my back creak as I turn my body to face the staircase. The air that sucks into my nostrils is filled with nostalgia. It's the same smell that rolled through the kitchen windows and into my home this morning. The base of the stairs shimmers in a light red hue but with each step the color gradient shifts from maroon to golden white. The light grows brighter with each step toward it. I turn my neck and shoulders with every movement, scanning the perimeter. The shadow creature still lurks in my home. I don't know what it wants but it is consuming my mind and filling it with terror. The base of the stairs is at my feet and I look at every step as my vision climbs up slowly.

The air falls silent. I drop to my knees and all of the oxygen from within me is extinguished. At the top of the staircase is my mother and my brother. They stand side-by-side, motionless. The bright golden-white light shimmers behind them. "Mom... Will..." I utter with a croak. Warm air releases from my nostrils with every harsh exhale. The creaking of floorboards rings loudly. I turn my head and standing in the front doorway is the creature. It is totally black and lacks any sort of definition or features. Then, it opens its glowing red eyes. They are filled with pain and aggression and the veins climb along the sclera of its eyeballs.

"David, honey," my mom's angelic voice echoes.

Tears swell in my stinging eyes and I look to her with quivering lips. She stands by my little brother with her arm extended out by her hip. William gently grabs hold of her hand. They interlock and gaze down the staircase at me. I lean desperately against the steps and try to drag myself up. My arms shake violently as I pull myself along one step at a time. "I'm coming, mom," I exclaim. A thin, black hand wraps around my ankle and yanks me. The creature snarls and pulls me away. The golden lights shimmering above my mom and brother grow brighter and their bodies become less defined.

My nails scratch against the ground and I pull up the carpet as the demon drags me toward the front door. I scream and yell and extend my arms for my mother and brother. They turn and face the shimmering golden-white light atop the staircase. The light grows brighter, and they step right into it and out of my sight forever. Darkness rolls in from the second floor and washes over the golden illumination, drowning it and extinguishing the light. The waves of blackness rush toward me as I'm pulled along the brown carpet. The darkness engulfs my childhood home and right as I am pulled into an apocalyptic world, I close my eyes and let the night wash over me. I have no definition, no features, and nothing to hold onto. I'm cold and shivering, and all that remains is that nostalgic smell that awoke me. It lingers in the murky reality that I'm doomed to float through for the rest of my existence.

The Final Domino

The rain lashed against the aluminum roof. The pitter-patter of falling drops consumed the air inside the Gym. Thunder rattled every other moment and brief but bright flashes of light would shine through small windows high on the walls of the space. That day was my first time working in the laundry. I had signed up to help out in the laundry room. I had heard Markus was doing the same thing, and I wanted to finally have some time to talk to my old friend alone, and without the discomforting thought of being stabbed for associating with "an enemy." Eric understood that we all had friends outside the gang, but loyalty called for homogeneity. Joe did not get it, nor did the other dudes in my gang that slept in other pockets of the Gym. If these boys knew I was sneaking around behind their backs, they'd have me for dinner. I had to make sure that every display of affection I had for my brother was behind closed doors.

We entered the Gym from the yard parched and hungry. I smelled a familiar smell. It reminded me of my mother's cooking. I was salivating. We had some snacks lying around the pocket. Dinner wouldn't be for another few hours, at least. In that prison, honeybuns went for $3. I understood it as inflation. Perhaps it was just the institution trying to squeeze a buck out of us. The brightness of day quickly turned to gloom as we walked to the beginning of our aisle.

"Yo' Dave, bring us back some fresh sheets today, huh?" Joe said while holding his GED book tightly. "All right," I responded. My eyes moved toward the direction of my bunk. I could see someone by it, lingering. They had their backs turned at first, but they were white.

"Yo, you see that?" I asked.

Joe and Eric looked. Their eyes grew wide. Eric stopped in his tracks and Joe stood forward. Other incoming inmates from the yard passed us by and rubbed shoulders aggressively with me and Eric. "I know who that motherfucker is," Joe exclaimed as he stopped. The man turned around. Jamie stood before us with a healing black eye and a look of isolation on his dreary face. He was wearing a dirty wife beater and had the torso of his orange overalls rolled down to the waist. Time slowed down. The beating of my heart seemed out of tune with reality. Then, everything sped up suddenly.

"Yo, what the fuck is you doin' to my bunk, cracker?" Joe yelled at the top of his lungs.

Jamie lifted his head and sprinted toward his own pocket. He squeezed in with the other white men that were there and Joe stopped with a skid in the middle of the aisle. "Jamal was my fucking homie. I'm gonna fucking kill you one day, I hope you know that," Joe screamed out. Everyone turned to face the commotion, even the guards. I could see them hovering their hands over their batons. Jamie stuck his head out through his pack. His own guys were clearly reluctant to protect him but race is above all in prison. Out of respect for the color of their skin, they did what they had to do at that moment, even though they wanted him dead more than anybody else. I thought they were going to do it, too. I wouldn't have predicted Jamie to survive more than 48 hours after his excommunication in the yard.

"Anybody that throws a single punch is going in the hole for a month... Go back to your bunks," a guard yelled out.

I didn't know any of the guards. Unlike my previous experience, the Gym was cold. The guards were stone-faced and rarely, if ever, engaged in communication with an inmate. At least O'Bannion let things slide and there was mutual respect. The men and women who patrolled the Gym were quiet, the polar opposite of O'Bannion. Their eyes never closed. Every step they took was careful and calculated, always ensuring they had a solid center of gravity in case a physical altercation were to suddenly break out. A lot of dudes in prison talked about other institutions they had been to and how they were different from the Gym. We all had stories. Eric was locked up in some place down south near the border of Mexico and he claimed that he used to get off with some of the female guards. He said that they would come on to him and offer up their bodies in exchange for drugs that Eric and other guys from our gang would import. Eric had a whole scheme where these guards would bring the drugs in themselves, hand them off to Eric in his cell, fuck him, and then take their small share of narcotics while turning a blind eye to the fact that the rest of the drugs were going to be sold and used within confines of the prison walls. I didn't have a scheme like that in the Gym, virtually nobody did.

"What was that white motherfucker doing over here?" Joe pondered to himself as he rooted around his own bunk.

"I'll be back in a few hours. Make sure nobody else fucks with our shit," I said to Eric and Joe as I slipped my phone under my pillow and stepped away from our pocket.

It was time. I was led through hallways by two silent and stern guards. I didn't pipe up or run my mouth. I was smarter than that. A guard would approach you anyway if they wanted something.

Engaging with one without any basis of benefit for their party could have meant serious reprimand that would have ensured I stayed behind bars for the rest of my life. Joe and Eric had me thinking about parole. My time was coming a handful of years down the line and I knew that I didn't want to be in prison forever. I realized that my psyche couldn't take it. Every day was a battle and I was strong, but every man had their breaking point and for me, it was my dreams that showed the mental cracks in my life. My conscience weighed heavy from the slew of nightmares that were consuming my mind and eating my brain from the inside out. I could feel the incoming disaster. I sensed the onslaught of a doomed existence and there was nothing I could do but keep quiet and wait. It was important to me that I constantly reminded myself of outcomes. If I did X, then Y would happen. That's how I saw it.

"Through here. Officer Jacob will show you where you go," one of the guards said as he opened a giant steel door.

The sound of rattling laundry machines filled the air. The humming vibration of clothes and sheets swirling inside was constant and monotone. I could see Markus folding fresh orange overalls into a pile on top of a sleek metallic table. Two Asian dudes were clearly in charge of taking the dirty clothes and shoving them into the washers, and two skinhead white guys were responsible for taking the wet clothes out and moving them into the dryer. My head scanned the room and stopped upon seeing Jamie. It was his duty to take the dry clothes from the machine over to the table for Markus to fold.

"Are you David Spivey?" Officer Jacob yelled out like a drill sergeant.

"Yeah," I responded.

"It's either 'yes officer' or 'yes sir'. If I hear you say 'yeah' to me one more time I'll throw you in the box for fun. You understand, boy?"

"Yes, officer."

"You're folding jumpsuits with the other black. Now go on," Jacob exclaimed and pointed toward Markus.

I stood silently beside Markus as Jacob watched me like a hawk. His eyes scanned my body from shoes to hair. His hands were grasped together behind his back and he puffed his chest out. He was a body, but any one of us inmates could have taken him. You could tell when somebody lacked that true killer instinct. Jacob knew how to lift a weight, but if push ever came to shove, I'd put that motherfucker in the box without breaking a sweat.

"Dude's a fucking asshole," Markus whispered to me.

"What's his deal?"

"I heard some whispers that his wife left him for a black dude. He ain't ever got over it," Markus said as he folded laundry with a smile.

I grew up on the streets of Los Angeles, but I was raised a Southern boy. My mom and everyone else in her family tree sprouted out of the Deep South. My aunts and uncles all held a raging hate toward white folk. My mother was the only one who didn't, and it was because of her that I was able to tolerate behaviors that most of my black brothers and sisters could not. I always thought that if you could understand something, you could overcome it. That was how I felt about prison. I was determined to understand it. Inmates were moving cogs within the machine that is the institution. Knowing what each part did could help you understand how the machine operated as a whole. That's why there was something I desperately needed to hear Markus say.

"Can I ask you something, brother?"

"Sure," Markus responded.

"What are you in here for?"

"Why you askin' me that, Dave?"

"Come on, man. You know what I did. Everybody from the neighborhood knows what I did... Just tell me what you did. Nobody seems to know," I said with gentle sincerity.

Markus stopped folding for a moment. His head hung low and he did not blink. The rattling washing machines rumbled in their place behind us. "I'm here for murder, Dave. Everyone in the Gym is a killer. That's why all of us are the ones selected to live there and not in the cells like the rest of the inmates... We're the lowest of the low, man. So, you ask me what I did to get here and I'm telling you that you and I did the exact same thing that everyone else did. Ain't no reason to talk about it..." I was taken aback. Markus resumed folding the laundry on the metallic table. I joined in and we worked in silence.

"I'm sorry, man, I didn't think you'd mind me asking," I said.

"I don't mind. I only need to tell you once," he responded.

Jamie set some dry sheets on the metallic table and stood there for a moment. Our gaze caught each other. The bruising around his eye was more apparent at close range. He was beaten real good, probably multiple times over a few days. He looked weak and thin and his eyes were dreaming of the night they'd be able to rest without staying awake with a sting.

"Keep your ass working, Jamie, or else I'll send you back to the Gym," Jacob yelled out.

Jamie fled toward the dryers. Markus and I folded the sheets in silence. "You think there's any way I can get two sheets out of here without Hitler seeing?" I asked. Markus chuckled. His body shook. He wanted to let the laughter out more, but Officer Jacob had his eyes on us. "I'd like to see you try," Markus whispered. It was like we were seven years old again at Auntie Cheryl's house. We were just kids, man. We thought everything was hilarious and we wanted everyone to see what we saw. The walls that surrounded us couldn't squash that feeling. Our bond was much stronger than that. It was hard to believe that before that moment, we hadn't properly spoken to each other in years.

"Dave," a voice whispered.

I turned and standing before me was Jamie with his arms dangling down by his sides. "What the hell are you doing? Jacob's gonna' kick us both outta here if you don't stop foolin'," I whispered aggressively. Jamie took one step closer. I lifted my hand and opened my palm. "I'll fucking DP you if I have to, motherfucker," I said even more harshly. Jamie stopped several feet before me. He lifted his arm and pointed over my shoulder. I cautiously turned and my eyes widened upon seeing the doorway empty. Officer Jacob had stepped out.

"I need to talk to you before he gets back," Jamie said.

"Get the fuck out of here, man. You've got the golden touch of death. Whoever you're near gets slashed in the same movement that you do," Markus said.

"Please Dave," Jamie said as he ignored Markus and looked at me with big, sad eyes.

"You got sixty seconds."

Jamie took a deep breath and quickly looked at the floor. Markus and I stood tall before him as he conjured up his words. Then, he lifted his head and out they came in a passionate flow; "I knew Jamal. We worked together in the kitchen for two years. He was my best friend.

Nobody else knew that. We even had our own way of talking. We only had a few hours together each day and both of us knew that it wasn't enough, so we started to learn a little sign language so we could communicate from across the Gym. We frequently talked about the days when we'd be free and back out on the streets. He wanted to open a bar and I agreed to help him. I don't have any skills, I know that. He was going to lead us both to success... One morning, Jamal signaled that he was afraid. He said that he owed the Asians some money. I told him I didn't have any, but I had a shiv that he could trade for more time while he figured out a way to get the chili. So, I walked over to his bunk and as I was about to set the shiv down, Joe saw me and swatted me away. I was never able to drop it for Jamal. Later that night, he went to the Asians to bargain and Tyler punctured him with a butter knife. He held his hands tightly over the wound and instead of stumbling back to his pocket or even to a guard, he came to me. He begged for help with a whisper and then he removed his hands from his wound and blood spilled out onto the floor of my pocket. He told me that if he died in my arms, then I'd be dead before the sun rose. So, he pushed himself free and into the aisle. He dragged himself along the Gym floor, leaving a trail of blood behind. Inmates started to awaken and turn to look at him as he groaned with struggle during each movement. He pulled himself into bed and died… The lights came on and the trail of blood and guts led right back to me. I could see Joe's stare burning a hole in my sockets. His eyes were red and his gaze was unforgiving... I didn't expect to be alive this long, but I know what Joe is plotting. I know he thinks that I killed his friend, and I know that the moment he catches me alone will be the last moment I ever take a breath in. I don't know what I'm waiting for, really..."

"Well, what do you want from me?" I responded.

"I just wanted somebody... anybody to know that before the inevitable happens," Jamie said before being interrupted by Jacob.

"Jamie, if I have to tell your ass one more time!"

Jamie scurried back to the dryer. Markus and I turned to each other in silence. "The same goes for the blacks. Got that?" Jacob said to me and Markus as our backs were faced toward him. The shift ran for another couple of hours. Markus and I were the last ones to leave. We had dozens of sheets to fold and stock into a cart. It was the duty of another inmate to delegate the freshly washed sheets and overalls throughout the entire Gym. I couldn't get any out. That guy hadn't even shown up yet. Officer Jacob stood by the door like a bouncer. "I'm happy we're both doing this, Dave," Markus whispered. "You're like a piece of home," he followed. He was the same to me. He gave me that feeling of nostalgic warmth that my mom and brother emitted. It was time to go back to the Gym.

Officer Jacob strutted forward with his back upright and his chest puffed out. He tapped his fingers on the base of his baton and whistled a white folk tune. Markus and I sauntered behind him and smirked at each other every other moment. Jacob opened the doors for us and didn't bother looking us in the eye as he gestured for us to enter. He shut the door behind us and locked it before stalking the perimeter of the Gym and scanning the room for criminal activity like the other guards were. Markus and I split off. He went back to his gang, and I returned to mine.

Joe sat on the top bunk with his legs dangling over the edge. His phone was in his hand at first, but he carefully slipped it into his pocket as the seconds passed. His eyes were barely open, and his GED book was flipped upside down on his pillow. "Get off your phone, Joe. You got your test in two weeks," Joe mumbled to himself. Eric lay on his bed, texting his girl. He had a smile on his face. I think she was sending him dirty pictures. "You get me a date with Nadine yet?" I asked as I sat on my bunk. Eric set his phone down on his chest and turned his head to face me. "You get me my sheets yet, motherfucker?" I shook my head and pointed at Jacob as he trailed the walls. "Come on, Dave. You're a criminal. Be smart and figure it out next time, okay? I'll set up a date between you and Nadine after that happens. I promise," Eric exclaimed. I nodded in agreement. Joe hadn't even bothered to gaze in my direction. I don't think he even heard a word of that conversation.

"You good, Joe?" I asked.

"Look at that motherfucker..." Joe mumbled.

That sinking feeling in my stomach returned. Jamie was at the top of our aisle, and he was mindlessly strolling down it and toward our pocket. His hands were behind his back and his head was hung low. Joe carefully reached under his pillow and I could see him grabbing hold of a shiv. His fingers wrapped around the base of the weapon as he slipped out and hid it under his hands atop his lap.

"If that cracker comes within two feet of me, he's dead," Joe muttered as his eyes continued to gaze at the approaching Jamie.

I stood to my feet. Eric did, too. I even met Markus' gaze from across the room and he was staring right back at me. "You've got your test soon, man. You pass it, and at your parole hearing, they're gonna let you go because you showed them you want to get better. Don't blow it," I said. He didn't listen. He took slow and careful breaths and readied himself for war. Jamie was strolling down the aisle. His lips quivered and his cheeks gently shook. More heads started to turn to watch as he walked by. Then, he stopped.

"Oh no," I whispered.

Jamie stood before Tyler's bunk. He had his hands behind his back. They were clenched into fists and veins popped out from his forearms. "Tyler," Jamie said. Tyler remained still as he lay down. Only his eyeballs moved. "I'm talking to you, motherfucker," Jamie followed. A smirk grew on Tyler's face. He swung his legs and sat up on his bunk before reaching into his pocket and pulling out a small spoon and a bag of cocaine.

"What the fuck do you want?"

Tyler scooped cocaine out of the bag and into the indent of his small spoon. He lifted it to his nose and snorted it. His head shook around and he clenched his eyes closed as the coke shot up into his brain. Jamie stood there watching him, and the rest of us lay silent with our gaze focused on them. Tyler lifted his gaze to meet Jamie's once more. He had a smile on his face and his yellow teeth were showing.

"Seriously, are you looking for trouble, man?" Tyler exclaimed. Jamie remained silent as he crouched down to be at the same eye level. Tyler scooped another spoonful of cocaine from the bag and held it right under his left nostril.

"I know you killed Jamal," Jamie whispered.

Jamie swung his arm out from behind his back and smashed his fist into Tyler's hand that held the snorting device. The cocaine spoon shoved right into Tyler's left nostril and blood immediately began to pour out as the object stuck out from the flesh inside the nose cave. Tyler jumped to his feet and screamed as he grabbed his reddening cheeks. The other three Asian gangsters in the pocket shot up to their feet and their eyes sprung wide open. Jamie sprinted down the aisle, right toward my pocket. Officer Jacob blew his whistle and yelled out "Everybody stays fucking still!"

Joe gripped his shiv tightly and jumped down to the ground. Jamie was running right for us down the aisle. Three Asians rushed behind him, and just beyond that, Jacob and two of his guards trailed. My heart beat fast. My gaze constantly switched between Jamie and Joe. The dirty steel of the shiv poked out from Joe's perspiring hand. Jamie grew closer, and closer, and closer, and right as he stepped into our pocket I sprung from my bunk and tackled Joe to the ground. His shiv went skidding across the floor and Jamie whizzed by the pocket with his neck turned 90 degrees to look at me on the floor. He was expecting to die, and instead, he was tackled by a guard that popped out from behind a bunk. Jacob whipped out his gun right by my bunk and fired a warning shot into the ceiling. Rain started to pour in through the hole in the aluminum and splatter down into the aisle adjacent to my bed. "You gooks slam the brakes or else the next one is in your spine," Jacob screamed. The three Asians immediately threw their hands into the air.

Jamie was pinned to the floor and had the handcuffs slapped on his wrists. The touch of steel was all too familiar. He was dragged to his feet and immediately taken out of the Gym and brought right to the hole. I had heard sometime later that he spent three months in there, only to be slashed in the throat the day he came back to the Gym. Nobody knows who did it. It could have been Tyler, or it could have been his own gang. I guess it also could have been Joe, but he managed to pass his GED and get approved for parole not too long after.

While the commotion was settling and the Asians were being reprimanded by Jacob, I could feel the vibration of my phone buzzing from beneath my pillow. Jacob was only ten feet from my bunk. It was a risky move, but for some reason, my gut told me to look. I carefully slipped my hand underneath my pillow. Eric looked at me and shook his head, but I didn't listen. I could feel the cold metal of my phone's exterior against my wet fingertips. The buzzing stopped as I touched it. The pillow became a barrier from Jacob's sight and I opened my phone with a flip. The screen illuminated my face with a gentle blue light and the bright white lettering spelled out; "One unheard voicemail from MOMMA." I lay on my stomach with my ear pressed against the speaker of the phone and I clicked play.

"David, honey, this is your aunt Shanice. I tried figuring out how to get in touch with you as fast as possible, but that jail you're in moves too slow, so I asked if I could go through your mother's phone before they split up her possessions... I don't know how to say this, baby, but something real bad happened. Your, uh, your mom passed, honey... And, and... William... Some guys from a different neighborhood gang, they, uh... I'm so sorry, baby... We all tried to get the message to you as quickly as possible..."

The cold blue light shone onto my face as I slowly pulled my head away from my phone. My thoughts halted, and my arms and fingers shook. "Yo' Dave, put that fucking phone away before Jacob sees you," Eric whispered. The walls started to shake. The hairs on my neck stood upright. Violent strikes of lightning sparked in my mind and they were followed by the paralyzing rumble of thunder. I shot to my feet and put my hands over my eyes. My muscles contracted and retracted as if I were being swapped between an oven and a freezer. My lungs struggled to fill with air and my nose tingled with the sensation of an onslaught of tears and snot. Eric grabbed my wrist but I ripped myself free from his grasp. My red, watering eyes became known, and Eric dropped his arms to his side. Tears streamed down my shaking cheeks. My knees felt weak like I was going to fall to the cold ground at any moment.

"FUCK!" I screamed at the top of my lungs.

Every single head in the Gym turned to face me as I bawled my eyes out. Even the Asians who were pinned to the ground and handcuffed were watching me. Eric tried pulling me in once more, but I turned and ripped myself free from his gasp once again. Officer Jacob stood to his feet with a curious twitch in his neck. He carefully approached my pocket. Eric's gaze shot down to the illuminated cell phone that was clearly visible atop my bed. "Dave, your phone," he whispered to me. I couldn't hear him. My mind couldn't focus on anything that wasn't my mother or brother. I yearned for their touch and for their voice. My spine felt like gelatin and my head was consumed by bats that fluttered their wings and crashed into the walls of my cranium.

Eric jumped across the pocket and landed on the phone atop my bed right as Officer Jacob approached us. "Are you trying to find a way into the hole, Spivey?" Jacob asked. I didn't respond. My legs and arms shook and tears rolled down my steaming hot face. "He just found out his mom died. That's what it is," Eric said as he lay on my bed. The entire Gym was silent. Only my sniffles would fill the air every other moment. Jacob tilted his head as he looked down at Eric. "What have you got there, Eric?" Jacob asked as he forcefully ripped Eric up off the bed. My cell phone fell to the floor right between the officer's feet. Joe's eyes shot wide and he turned to me. Jacob tutted and shook his head. "Is this your phone, Eric?" Jacob asked. I wanted to open my mouth but I could not find words from even the deepest pits inside of me.

"Yeah," Eric responded.

"Yeah? Don't you think an officer with the power to make your life hell deserves a better answer than "yeah"?" Officer Jacob repeated as he gripped his baton.

"You heard me," Eric responded.

Jacob smiled, then took a deep breath. "If that's what you want," Jacob said as he smashed the cell phone with a powerful blow from the sole of his booted foot. The pieces went flying and skidding all over the Gym. "Round up the gooks, take em to the hole, and let's try this whole thing again," Jacob yelled out to the other guards.

The guards left with the inmates, but all heads were still aimed in my direction. I turned to Eric and tried to muster up the words, but they still were held captive by my emotions. "I'm a lifer, man. I'll never leave the prison system. You still got a chance to get out of here, and to do that you need a clean record," Eric exclaimed as my mouth hung open. "I never want to see you and Joe within these walls again. You both got that? Eric followed as he looked at us before he extended his hand to me and I grasped it with a shake that started in my shoulder and ran down my arm. "Thank you," I said with a croak in my voice.

I gently slipped my hand free from Eric's grasp. I knew he was always going to be okay. He was stronger than the rest of us and he had respect. The man could do no wrong, but unfortunately, in prison that doesn't matter. He was going to have to fight for the rest of his days, and I always thought that I bore some responsibility.

I swung my sight toward Markus. He was gazing right at me. Everything else was dark and shadowy. The only light that shone from above reigned down on Markus. I jumped out of my bunk and paced down the aisle. Heads and eyes scanned me as I whizzed by them with tears rolling down my cheeks and vulnerability emitting from my pores. My breathing was sharp and long but I did not care. I walked right into Markus' pocket and wrapped my arms around him. My enemies watched as two childhood friends embraced each other with their eyes closed.

Markus made it out of the Gym and into a two-man cell a few months after I left. His record remained clean and his mind was as untouched as an incarcerated gang member's could be. I knew at that moment that my time in the Gym, and Northern California, was over. The next few years, man, they just flew by. I couldn't think about a single thing other than my mom and my brother. I psychologically whipped myself and tortured the remaining humanity within me for not being there. I was on the inside because of my own doing, and they were on the outside paying for my sins. I couldn't even begin to think about what their final thoughts were. Reality did not exist for me during my darkest years. I moved from institution to institution, year after year, selling drugs to people I trusted and hanging with my allies. I was a living ghost that nobody could see. I never stepped out of line in the eyes of the streets or the eyes of the guards. I walked that fine line with a bleeding heart, and I never found comfort as I did with Star, Eric, or Markus. My life accelerated to a speed at which I could not see and before I knew it I was in my twelfth year of incarceration and I had become a man and was no longer a boy. Parole was just a few years away, and I still had a clean record, despite the numerous hurdles that were thrown before me in my race to freedom. I would not let my mother and brother die in vain.

Room Number 15

The smoke dissipates and the glowing lights of the Hollywood Park Motel shimmer in the distance like an oasis in the desert. I stand in darkness. Dotted yellow lines run along the street and through the gap in my feet. The cold butt of a gun is grasped in my sweaty hand. The barrel slowly exerts steam. It rises up along my shirt and into my nostrils and the pungent odor of gunpowder slinks its way to my brain. The whispers of moaning men and women echo throughout the air. The sounds are coming from the motel.

The atmosphere is cold. My toes cling together like penguins in the Antarctic during a winter storm. I try to separate them but my bones feel weak and ready to snap at any moment. Walking is difficult. Everything is dark. The illumination of the motel is my only guiding light. The closer I get to the structure, the more defined it becomes. There is a red pickup truck parked outside the lobby, which sits at the front of the motel, closest to the sidewalk. The building is long and thin and runs far back. Fifteen red doors back to be exact. Each one is the same as the next.

The windows of the lobby are condensed. Droplets of water run down them from the inside. I stand on my tip-toes and I try to peer through the glass but the haze is too thick. I can't make out a single object. "Hello?" I yell as I tap on the window with my gun. No response. The air is dead and not even the wind makes itself known. I turn to face the red pickup truck. It purrs. I open the passenger side door and the keys dangle from the ignition, clinking and clanking together to create a soft jingle. I pull them out but the engine continues to run. The keys are warm to touch and the keychain has an indent of the symbol of my enemies. I toss them into the cup holder and slam the door shut.

"Is anybody here?" I yell out as I slip my pistol into my waistband.

Door number 2. I approach it with a shake in my step and I grab the knob with a full grasp. The palm of my hand sizzles against it and I rip my arm away. Steam rises from the burn. "Motherfucker," I mumble to myself. The chilling blue moon casts cyan rays down onto my face as I ponder my next move. I look down to my boots. The soles are made from thick rubber. I take two steps back and lunge forward with my leg held high and knee bent. The wood of the door cracks down the middle as I put my foot through it. Splinters spray into the dark room and I poke my head through. "Hello?" I yell into the blackness. There's nothing here. There is no bed, no TV, no definition of any object. It's just darkness, empty space that will suck me in and exhaust me of my life.

The sharp noise of crashing metallic trash cans suddenly pierces my eardrums. I whip my head left and gaze down the stretch of red doorways. A spinning metal lid swirls in the center of the lot before coming to a silent halt. There is nothing else. The glow of the motel only extends so far out into the parking lot before a wall of darkness blocks the rest of reality from my sight. It's everlasting and ominous in size and stature. I gently walk toward the tin cap sitting atop the cement. There are bullet holes in it. The shots cleaned right through the substance. I lift the circular object and hold the gaps up to my eye line. I peek through them like a pair of binoculars.

"David," a croaking voice echoes.

The metallic lid crashes against the ground as it slips through my perspiring hands and falls at my feet. It spins like a quarter on the cement. It makes this swirling noise that I fear will never silence. I turn my head and briefly spot the silhouette of a man shifting through the opened entrance of Room 15 and slam the door behind him. The butt of my pistol is cold as I grip it and hold it out from my chest. My heart beats slowly and air rushes out from my nostrils as I walk toward the end of the motel stretch. Muffled sounds of laughter ring through me. I gulp. The saliva scratches against my esophagus as it slides down into my stomach where the acid bubbles and burns anything it touches.

My boot is raised high off the ground. My shadow stretches long and far and engulfs areas of brightness into darkness. I slam my foot through the red wooden door and it creates a hole. A cold and muted green reflection shines through it and out into the lot. I crouch down to it and peak. My eyes shoot wide open and I jolt immediately back upright. I ram my shoulder into the door over and over and over. The frame rattles in place and the screws and bolts shake and dance before slipping out of their pockets and clank against the cement below. Bruising appears on my bicep but I continue on my mission until the door finally breaks free from its hinge and slams flat onto the carpeted floor. I stand tall with heavy breaths. My chest puffs out and retracts back with every ounce of air I swallow into my lungs.

A trail of blood slithers between my feet. It stains the carpet a dark red. I follow the line until I see the hand of a teenage black boy. His head is turned to face away from me, but I know who it is. I can hardly stand the sight of him. His flesh is open and life pours out from his wounds. The bed is made and the bedspread covers the entire mattress. Two lumps are resting beneath it. Sticking out at the end of the silk sheet are two pairs of feet. One of them has painted pink toenails, and the other is coarse and has scratched soles. My heart thumps. The smell of nostalgia slinks into my nostrils and warm air caresses my body. The floorboards beneath the carpet creak as I carefully step toward the board of the bed. Blood drips down the sides of the cot and creates pools in the carpet below. I grab a hold of the bedding and right as I am about to rip it back I hear the clattering of shampoo bottles and falling razors in the bathroom.

The door is ajar and a blue color shines from within the bathroom. It meshes with the green lights of the bedroom and displays a thin wall of teal blotches of light that swarm through the air like bubbles in a lava lamp. I extend myself into it and experience a short sense of euphoria along the edges of my spine as I push the brown door open and enter. In my peripheral vision, I spot the shower curtain shaking. There is someone on the other side. I carefully slide my finger onto the trigger and I use my other hand to grab ahold of the plastic sheet. My breaths are short and sharp and my eyes sting. A pain rumbles in my head that will not cease. It feels like there is a bug digging its way into my brain. I close my eyes for just a moment, and then I rip the sheets open and blindly fire a shot. The flash fills the room with a bright white light and as the dimness sets in I open my eyes and choke on my spit as I look at the bloody body of a black boy strewn out in the tub. Blood drains with a hypnotic swirl. I pull the barrier back to hide the murder and I burst out of the bathroom with heavy breaths and a pounding heart.

The twenty toes and four ankles of the mysterious bodies catch my sight again and the air stands still. The humps under the sheets are ones that I've seen before. A sadness bubbles from deep inside the acid of my stomach and I puke a black sludge right onto the carpet. It sizzles and burns the wool and sinks through the floorboards and straight down to the core of the earth. The broken red pieces of wood litter the bloody room and a wall of mist flows from the parking lot outside and into the air I breathe. I have to know who is under the covers. I need to understand why they are there and who did this to them, but I'm afraid. I fear for my life with every step and with each breath. Emotions creep through every dark crevice of my existence and inhibit the feeling I had as a boy when my mother reprimanded me for misbehaving. The nostalgia eats me away from the inside. None of this makes sense.

The sheets are cold to the touch. I grip hold of the silk and I rip it back with all of my might. A breeze washes over me and flows through the room. The atmosphere is silent. My eyes are wide and filled with tears. The familiar faces of my fallen family lay before me with their arms pointed straight and down by their sides. Their lips are sewed shut and their solid white eyes are wide open and without pupils. Their skin has a blue touch to it and I can't bear to look any longer. I turn my head. The bones in my neck creak and crack loudly for the world to hear. The pain is too great and I don't know how to make it better.

A dark and deep laughter rumbles from within the fog and shakes the motel. The mist drifts into the room and hangs in suspension as it circumnavigates the space. My vision dulls and the once-green hue that illuminated the room has been swallowed by gray. I now stand alone in a barren wasteland, unable to see two feet ahead of me. The chilling air freezes my lungs. I fear that my next breath will be my last.

Predators & Prey

After 12 years, I was still just a murderer. My actions had caused a chain reaction. My mom and my brother were dead because of me. That's what I told myself every morning, noon, and night. Even my subconscious called me a killer. I couldn't escape it. Life had become a blur by the time I entered my final prison. The institution was about 80 miles from Los Angeles. It was the closest to home I had been in a long time. The nearest city was Bakersfield and sometimes I could hear the cars whizzing by on the streets late at night. A younger man would have gone crazy, but to a seasoned inmate, it was all white noise. It all blended with the natural sounds of the environment.

I stood in a long line of inmates as I waited for my name to be called. It was the same old story. Nothing would be different than my previous experiences. Violence ran supreme and the guards were constantly at war with the inmates. It was considered to be the most deadly institution in California. I knew I had to watch my six at all times, but standing there in that line, I didn't see the point. The walls were thick and impenetrable and all I wanted was to see the other side. I owed my mom and brother that much. I couldn't go the rest of my life without seeing their headstones side-by-side. The thought of the LA sun reigning high above the cemetery and cooking the ground in which they lay caused irritations in my brain. I knew I had to at least try to get out, and it all started with my mindset.

My eyes looked at my black shoes and the bottoms of my dirty orange overalls. I was sick of that sight. My skin may well have been orange by that point. The clothes were a part of me and I was constantly reminded of the horrific murder all those years ago at the Hollywood Park Motel. I couldn't get the image out of my mind. I guess that was the point. The sounds of shifting inmates in the line in which I stood were muffled. I just didn't care. Name after name was called and every other moment I would take a step forward waiting to be delegated to a cell so I could just rest my eyes. We were like cows being readied for slaughter. I existed in a trance until I heard a name called that brought me right back to reality. The whiplash snapped me awake and I swung my head up to see that decrepit, foul fucking rapist with my own eyes once more.

"Anthony Jackson," the guard yelled.

"It's Puma, motherfucker."

Puma stood tall at the top of the line. There were strands of gray in his afro and the back of his neck had been all sliced up. His muscles had grown and he held more weight. I wanted to see his face. He towered over the rest of us inmates in that line. My stomach growled. The acid within bubbled and sizzled a heat inside me. My eyes were focused on his broad shoulders. His orange jumpsuit was pinned tightly to him. The definition of his back was projected through the polyester. "Cellblock 2. Officer Terry will show you there," the guard said.

Officer Terry was a small, white man with freckles on his cheeks and a thin neck that lacked muscle definition. He was a shrimp. The man would be eaten alive without that badge. Puma turned and I could see his side profile as he smirked at the puny guard. There were indents on his face like craters that had been carved by knives. His lips were cracked and chapped and I could see the pink flesh in every slash. The man was a walking relic. He had seen the inside of prisons all over the state for the majority of his life. He knew he was never getting out so he didn't bother to hold anything in.

"You ever had a dick in your ass, Officer Terry? You damn look like you have, you motherfuckin' pussy," Puma boomed as he stood tall over Terry.

"I'm a CO, boy. Watch your mouth," Officer Terry responded.

Puma took a step closer and his shadow swallowed Terry whole. The light cast from the flickering bulbs above had dimmed and Terry's eyes were wide. The running water through the pipes above and below hummed as the rest of us inmates could only stand by and watch the power shift from guard to inmate. Terry was shaken in his place, and he would have crumbled if not for two fellow guards who slammed their batons against a metal beam. The echo ran along the walls and sent sharp clangs into my eardrums. Puma didn't even flinch. He slowly turned to face the line he stood at the top of and he smiled. His teeth were not all there, and the ones that were were yellow and brown. I could practically smell his breath. My gaze caught his, and his found mine. He lifted his chained hands and saluted me before being dragged away.

I was told that I would be designated a two-person cell in Block 2. I was happy that I was not in the same quarters as Puma, but it didn't really matter. That fucking rapist would be slithering his way around the yard every single day. Officer Terry personally led me. He stopped and removed the keys from his waistband as he stood outside my new home. He immediately and accidentally dropped them onto the cold metal grated floor. He picked them up and the keys clinked together with a jingle. "You're one clumsy motherfucker, Terry," a high-pitched voice squealed from inside the cell. Terry didn't respond. He stuck a key into the lock and twisted it with his whole arm. "All right, Spivey. Get in," he said to me. My boots thumped against the metal floor as I approached the cell. The bars became visible first and as I stood before them I caught a glimpse of my new cellie. He was short but buff. His immaturity was apparent. His body moved up and down as he did push-ups in the middle of the room. There was a TV that played Jeopardy, a boombox that was switched off, a fine carpet, and a synthetic candle that smelled like maple.

"This is Romeo. You boys play nice," Officer Terry said as he gripped hold of one of the bars on the cell door.

"Hold on a second, Terry," Romeo said as he stood to his feet and wiped the sweat from his forehead. He walked right by me and pulled out a small wooden box from under his bed. There must have been two grand inside. He licked the tips of his fingers and he counted through hundred dollar bills with a whisper. Then, he slid the box back to its hiding hole and approached Terry with it all fanned out. He leaned against a bar and smirked. "I got the chili, but I'm waiting for the sauce, Terry," Romeo said. Terry gulped and looked over both of his shoulders. I stood there silently. "I'll have it tomorrow," Terry whispered. Romeo waggled his index finger and Terry leaned in. Romeo opened his mouth right by Terry's ear and whispered into it. I never did know what was spoken of, but Terry's eyes shot wide open, bloodshot. When Romeo finished with his demands Terry leaned back and silently nodded like a schoolboy who had been told off by his teacher.

"Okay Romeo," Terry said with a scratch in his throat, before turning and walking away.

Romeo turned to me and a fat smile smeared across his youthful face. He tossed his arms up into the air as if he were king giving a speech to a crowd of plebians. The ego was pungent. "Welcome," he yelled. I turned my back to him and looked around the decorated room. Only my bunk was untouched. Romeo stood by my side and put his arm around me but I pushed him away instantly. "What the fuck you think you're doing, man?" I said to him. That smile never left his face. He stared at me with wide eyes that never blinked. He was cracked out on something. "If we're gonna' make this work, you gotta trust me," he said. The boy was green. Anyone with any ounce of prison knowledge knew that trust was not cheap. It was not fast and unassumed. It took time to let someone into your life. The touch of another man usually only came with a violent blow.

"You only been inside for a few months, huh?" I asked.

"That easy to tell, huh?" he responded.

"You look green as a damn frog."

Romeo laughed hysterically. He threw his hand onto my shoulder and I swatted him away once more. He didn't flinch. Instead, he continued to laugh and approach his bunk. He slipped his hand under his mattress and pulled out a cell phone. "Here," Romeo said as he threw the device at me. It reminded me of my old one. It was the same model, but slightly newer and more expensive. I had heard the internet was quicker. "Nice phone. You're a lucky guy," I said. Romeo dropped to the floor and started doing push-ups.

"It's yours," he muttered with a shortness of breath. I flipped it open and a blue light shone onto my face.

"What's in it for you?" I asked.

"Your trust," he responded.

I had no choice. A phone was a major advantage, and I missed my brothers, especially Eric, Markus, and Star. I knew their numbers by heart and I typed them and saved the contacts. A smile struck my face. I had an idea. My fingertips felt sensitive as they rapidly pounded against the buttons. My text read; "I'm an hour's drive from LA and I think I remember you promising me a date with Nadine, motherfucker." The phone exerted a swooshing sound as I sent the text to Eric. It felt good to start the conversation again. In my last few institutions, I had to rent people's phones every other week so I could stay in touch with Star, Markus, and Eric. I powered off the device and slipped it under my pillow, then I lay on my back and stared up at the gray ceiling. I was getting real tired of that fucking view.

"I gotta give you the low down on this place, Dave," Romeo said.

"I've been incarcerated for twelve years, asshole. I don't need instructions," I said as I closed my eyes.

"You're not even curious about what I said to Terry?" Romeo asked.

My eyes opened and I turned to lie on my side. I looked at Romeo and he gazed back. He had a smile on his face. He crouched down to meet me at eye level. "I know you trust me, but I don't know if I trust you yet," he said brazenly. Romeo was an old-fashioned con artist at heart. He knew how to extract information from you and he would do it without you even realizing. I was a smart man, but even I was almost dragged down by the weight of his persuasion.

"What are you in here for? That's all I wanna know," he said.

"That's bullshit, man. Doesn't mean shit," I responded.

"I just wanna know if you're a rapist or a child killer or some shit, all right?"

"I'm in for murder, attempted murder, shooting an occupied dwelling, and conspiracy... You happy?"

A smile formed on Romeo's face and he suddenly clapped his hands together. "That's fuckin' sweet, rogue. You a cold-blooded killer, huh? I think we gonna be just fine," he loudly exclaimed. Romeo was affiliated with a gang out of East Palo Alto. Instead of saying" dude" or "man", they would say "rogue." That's how you knew if someone was from that neck of the woods.

"Now tell me about Terry," I demanded.

"Terry is my rat, my mule, and my punching bag. He does whatever I tell him to. When he's not working, he's out there scoring me heroin, weed, tobacco, coke, and perks. He brings them in and right to my cell and I don't even gotta pay him full price."

"How is that possible?"

"Let's just say I know some people who know where his family lives."

Romeo was going to get himself killed one day with that attitude. He hadn't spent long enough in prison to know that the power shifts are tectonic. They're unpredictable and have a powerful chain reaction that cannot be stopped with one pair of hands. I could feel the plates shifting beneath us, but it wasn't Romeo's time. He had the ego of a wicked prince and I knew in my gut that he was an aggressor in the yard. I had no choice but to stay loyal because he was one of us in here and we always banded together.

"There's some other shit you should know, too. You know, before we go to the yard," Romeo said.

"Like what?"

"This place is fiery, man, but we're the alphas. We're the ones who run shit. Me and JC, we're the kings of this kingdom... JC is like my little brother from another mother. You'll meet him in the yard, he's in Block 1."

"What about the guards?"

"I don't know most of them. They keep to themselves a lot of the time and let the inmates do their thing, unless someone does something right in front of them, then they're tough. Terry is my guy, you know that now. But, there is one that you should watch out for, because she'll put your ass in the box for a year without thinking twice... The bitch's name is Bailey," Romeo said.

Romeo would get me in trouble, and if I were going to aim for parole, then I couldn't risk being a liability. I would have to navigate it expertly. A lack of loyalty would have gotten me killed, and too much loyalty could have gotten me life. It took constant focus to keep your mind on the mission ahead. It required discipline, and as we walked out to the yard on my first day, I knew it would not come easy.

"This is Dave," Romeo yelled out to a group of young black men as we approached them in the yard. I was instantly but silently welcomed. The kids were big and I was their elder. I had never been in that situation until that moment. I was Eric to these fools. Philly, too. Dudes from my past that protected me and got in trouble for it. Now, it was those shoes that I wore and I feared they would be too big for my feet.

The yard was smaller than every other yard I had been to. There was a chain link fence around it. A basketball court occupied a lot of space in one corner. A gym with free weights occupied another area.

In our pocket in the dead center, we all stood tall. Some of the guys had knives on their person and a couple of them barely even tried to hide it. I was sweating bullets. "You need a knife, Dave?" Romeo asked. "Sure, but give it to me in the cell," I responded. Romeo laughed and nudged shoulders with JC. That boy was small, like a child. He was only nineteen years old. His blue eyes were weak. The boy was terrified and clung to Romeo like a helpless toddler.

"Tell JC about the Gym up north," Romeo demanded.

"I don't wanna talk about that shit, man," I responded.

"Come on, rogue," JC butted in.

"It was gruesome. They put hundreds of us all in one open room. We slept on bunk beds. Somebody died every so often. Guards watched us like we were caged animals. I'm happy I ain't there," I said sternly.

"Sounds fucking awesome," JC said with excitement. "Imagine slitting some cracker's throat in the middle of the night and getting away with it, rogue? That's the dream," he followed.

"How many bodies you rack up?" Romeo asked.

"None. I ain't stupid."

The smile was wiped from Romeo and JC's faces. I exhaled with a sigh and turned to them. "I got in plenty of fights, but nobody died. All right?" They were animals. Young, uneducated killers with a thirst for blood. I could see by the way groups in the yard moved that they were afraid of us. We were the aggressors, and the eyes of guards often found their way to that pocket of men in the center of the yard. I had been incarcerated for too long not to have picked up on the atmosphere that lingered in the air. I kept my mouth shut. I didn't want a display.

My gaze struck Puma as he sauntered across the open plain. The age was getting to him. He moved slower than usual, but the man still carried muscle. He was bigger than every other fool in there, but I seemed to be the only one who was aware of his reputation. "You see that dude?" I pointed at Puma. "The motherfucker with the afro?" Romeo responded as he pushed JC out of the way and stood by my side with a squint in his eye.

"That's Puma. You stay far away from him, you hear?" I said.

"Puma? Why's he called Puma?"

"Because he creeps up behind you. You don't hear him coming. He pounces on you and pins you down with all of his weight," I said before being interrupted.

"And then what, he rapes you?" Romeo butted in sarcastically.

"Trust me when I tell you that he is not someone to fuck with," I exclaimed.

Puma spotted us and walked toward our group. Romeo had that look in his eye. The kid definitely had plenty of DP's. "Let me do the talking," I said as I gently pushed Romeo back into the pocket. I walked several feet away from the group and Puma approached and stood before me. My neck leaned back slightly as I looked up to him. There was sharp, dry skin jutting out from his lips and his eyes were red and bloodshot. The scars on his cheeks looked to be old and healed as much as they could be. The air stood dead still for just a moment.

"What's good, Spivey?" Puma said with a smile.

"I got nothin to say to you," I responded.

Over Puma's shoulder, I spotted Officer Bailey. She stood upright and constantly had her arms down by her side. One hand hovered over her holster. The other gripped onto the top of a walkie which echoed static loudly into the air. She wore reflective sunglasses and had a ponytail to suppress the puffy curls on her head.

"I always liked you, Spivey. You know that?"

"Get the fuck out of here," I said sternly.

"Or what?" Puma exclaimed as he took a step toward me and his shadow engulfed my body in darkness.

Romeo burst out from the crowd. Veins were popping from his wrist as he held a shiv in his hand. He kept it low and out of Bailey's sight as he stepped toward Puma and me. My eyes jolted wide open when I saw it. I jumped in front of Puma and used my body as a shield. "Put that fucking thing away, Romeo," I voiced. He stood with the shiv pointed out at me. His head tilted to the side. "You told me yourself, this dude is trouble. He's got to go," Romeo uttered. Puma started laughing. Chills rolled up my spine. It amplified toxicity. My eardrums pounded inside me.

"I like your friends, Spivey. I'll see you guys around," Puma said before he licked his lips and strutted away.

"Put that fucking knife away before Bailey sees it, you idiot," I whispered to Romeo.

I was babysitting these fools. I didn't blame them for their behavior. I had a similar mindset when I was their age. I thought that violence and trouble would allow me to reach success but it was that mindset that was withholding me from achieving any sort of dream. JC, Romeo, and the boys all fucked around and did drugs for the remainder of the day. By the time we had returned to our cells and it was just Romeo and me, and we didn't speak. He was exhausted and crashed into his bed immediately. He left the TV on and episode after episode of Jeopardy continued to play throughout the night.

I lay in my bed at a quarter to two in the morning. I couldn't sleep. The light from the TV wasn't bothering me, nor was the static that very lightly sung in the air. My mattress vibrated. I rolled onto my side and ripped my phone out from under my bed. The screen projected white lettering that reflected in my eyeballs. It read; "One Message from Eric". I opened the text and a smile came across my face. No words, no hello, no goodbye, no how are you doing... It was just a number. Nadine's number. I called it instantly.

"Hello?" a soft voice spoke through the speaker.

"Yo' what's good, baby," I asked.

"Who the hell is this?" she said after a brief pause.

"Dave. Dave Spivey. Eric gave me your number."

"Oh, you're the boy who's been waitin' years to see me, huh?"

I stayed awake all night talking to Nadine. She was sweet and she understood the struggles I was facing. She didn't have any kids yet either. She was perfect, and it gave me another reason to try and get the fuck out of that place. I knew she would be the woman I was going to marry. I had to prepare for her first visit. I was going to look damn fine for her. I worked out in the yard every chance I got and even in my cell I would do sit-ups and push-ups to further define my abdomen. The prison was a lonely, isolating place. The warmth of a woman was what we all wanted even if we didn't admit it to each other. I considered myself lucky, and I counted down the seconds until I could set eyes on my love.

The First Date

Romeo's cackling laugh woke me up at six in the morning. He had a rerun of Family Feud playing on his television. My eyes were crusty when my lids opened. The soft, artificial illumination projecting from the TV cast blue lights onto my skin. Romeo hadn't slept that night. He stayed awake doing cocaine and texting his friends on the outside. He acted like a maniacal prince who could not be touched.

"Turn that shit down," I mumbled.

Romeo lazily picked up the remote and turned it down only two notches. I was ready to beat that boy's ass, but I didn't. I pretended to be asleep so I could think. I was seeing my girl Nadine that day and I needed to figure out what I was going to say to her. It was one thing texting and calling, but face-to-face, with guards watching your every move, was a whole different story. A lot of chicks from the neighborhood didn't mind dating an incarcerated man, but none of them actually wanted to marry one of us. Why would they? We couldn't touch them when we wanted, we couldn't work and put food on the table for them, and God forbid if you had a child with a girl on the outside, you couldn't be there for the kid. I knew it didn't make a whole lot of sense, but twelve years behind bars will rid you of your ego in ways you couldn't imagine. There was a woman who wanted to see me, and I was going to make sure I kept her.

My mind wandered in a purgatory-like existence as I slipped in and out of slumber. Heat crept along the hallways of the block and made its way into my cell. I could feel droplets of sweat forming on my forehead and dropping down to the pillow I rested my head upon. Footsteps echoed along the grated metal walkway outside. The steps grew louder and louder with every second that passed until they stopped. "Rising time, boys," Officer Terry's voice spoke. I rose in my bunk and turned to the guard on the other side of the bars. Romeo continued to watch TV.

"I don't want to talk to you until you've gotten me my sauce, Terry," Romeo said.

"Come on, Romeo. When have I ever missed a drop? I'll have it tonight. You boys gotta get to the cafeteria right now," Terry said.

"Nah," Romeo responded with his eyes still focused on the television.

I slipped on my clothes. Romeo kicked back even further. Terry gulped and leaned in closer to the bars. "I'm serious, Romeo. You can't stay in here," he said. Romeo cackled. I couldn't wait to get out of there. After breakfast, Nadine was going to be there. My shoes were tight as I placed my feet inside of them and I approached the cell door. The sounds of Family Feud filled the air as I looked at Terry, who gazed over at Romeo. Creaking and squealing metal rang with an echo as Terry swung the door open and entered the room.

"You can join the others outside in line, Dave," Terry said as he stood before Romeo.

"Don't talk to him like that," Romeo uttered.

"It's cool, Romeo. I'm hungry," I exclaimed.

I just got right out of the cell. I didn't want to be a part of whatever conversation was about to go down. Terry did his best to put on a strong face but we criminals know who has that dog in them and who does not. Officer Terry was a man who desperately wanted to be fierce but instead, he was inherently fearful. He succumbed to Romeo and as I stood in the line of inmates heading into the cafeteria he approached me and whispered into my ear.

"That kid is going to get you both killed," he said softly with a shake in his tone.

"Man, back the fuck up," I yelled.

Terry walked along the perimeter of the cafeteria as we all ate at metallic tables. Eggs, beans, and tortillas were our meal that morning. The chatter of inmates was loud and echoed in the room as noise bounced from steel wall to steel wall. JC sat next to me and kept quiet as he ate. Romeo was nowhere to be seen. I constantly lifted my head to look at the clock on the wall. One hour. My heart beat fast and I had no appetite. My mind had one thing on it. The hand clicked as it moved along the white face every second. Tick tock. The double doors opened. I whipped my head in that direction and I saw a large black man in a suit enter the cafeteria. He had a gray peppered beard and a short haircut. He looked like a square at first, until I noticed the tattoos on his neck and wrists. "Can I have everyone's attention for a moment?" he yelled out. The room went silent instantly. I wondered who the guy was. He was commanding and it seemed like he held the respect of a lot of the inmates.

"Yo' JC, who is that?" I asked.

"That's Earl. He's a counselor," JC responded.

Earl held himself like a CEO. He stood upright and cleared the phlegm from his throat. "I wanted to introduce myself yet again because I know we have a lot of new faces in here. My name is Earl, and I'm the prison counselor. My job is to talk with those of you who want to talk and help offer you advice. Now, I realize that many of you won't ever speak to me. That's fine. This is for the ones that know they need help... So, come see me if you've got something on your mind," he said eloquently.

"Only pussies talk to Earl," JC mumbled.

JC sounded like a fucking idiot. It reminded me of the way I acted when I was his age. Seventeen year old me would have said the same shit. Even though I had never used a counselor's services, I had grown to respect what they did. Parole was sneaking up, and I wanted to be ready. I watched as Earl stepped out of the cafeteria, and then everybody went straight back to chowing. The clock on the wall mocked me as the seconds passed by even slower. As soon as that bell rang, I could get up out of my seat, put my tray away, and get right to my girl.

My knee bounced as I watched the big hand strike twelve. It was the beginning of a new hour. The bell buzzed violently. I shot up from my seat, put my tray away, and got right in line. I knew that she was probably already there, waiting for me in the visitation room. I hoped that she looked like her pictures. There was a lot of noise in that line but I heard none of it. I wanted only one thing and nothing would break my focus. People started being filtered in. My turn was coming up. The clock's hands moved like molasses. My heart thumped. My toes curled and my spine felt a sensation of chills rushing up it. I was next, and Officer Terry nodded to me and opened the door to the visitation room.

A feeling rushed through me that I hadn't experienced since I was a teenage boy. She sat upright at a two-person table. She was facing me with big brown eyes and a smile. She had her nails done. They were long and pink. Her lipstick was precisely applied and her eyebrows had been plucked. The chick was serious. The touch of steel against my ass, as I sat in the chair, sent a shiver up my spine that complemented the beat of my heart. The words were trapped in my mouth and I just stared at her for a moment.

"Hey," she broke the ice with a smile.

"You're looking great. Fine as hell," I mustered up the courage to say.

"I could say the same thing to you."

This girl was sharp. She had wit. She sat in such a way that each and every curve on her body was showing. I was in, man. We made chit-chat for a little while, sizing each other up and testing where the boundaries were. "What's your opinion of Indian food?" I asked. "Nasty as hell," she responded. She was funny, and really stuck to her guns. I liked girls who were strong like that. It was electric right from the start. She would give it to me and I'd hit it right back. I wanted to jump over the table and grab her. I seriously almost risked it, but I had to stay restrained.

"I wish you weren't stuck in here," she said.

"I won't be for long, baby," I told her.

"You got a parole hearing coming up or something?"

"In about a year, yeah," I said confidently.

She was cute, man. A real dime. She had sex appeal, but she was motherly, too. She was a keeper, somebody I wanted to have around in my future. I saw it all with her. Her atmosphere was calming. I almost forgot that I wore orange overalls and black shoes. It felt like we were in the kitchen at a house party, learning about each other in rapid succession so we could justify the romance that would ensue.

"I know it's been some time, but Eric told me about your mom and your brother. I'm sorry," she said as she leaned across the table and rested her hand atop mine.

I wanted to rip myself free from those chains and wrap my arms around her and really just go at it. Instead, I thanked her. I was sold. She spoke about her past and explained to me that she was from a big family in South Central. She was the youngest of them all. Her parents were separated. They ripped apart right after she was born and she rarely saw her father. Her mother had cheated on him.

"That's fucked up," I said.

"It is what it is. She had needs," Nadine responded with a shrug.

The hour went by all too quickly. We had but a few minutes left before Officer Terry opened the doors for the civilians to flood out of. Nadine smiled at me and licked her lips. "I'd be all over you right now in better circumstances," she said seductively. "You don't even wanna know what I'd do to make that happen," I responded. She blushed. She was into me, big time. She told me so. She wanted to come back and visit as soon as she could. It was only about a two-hour drive for her on a good day, and three on a bad day. She was willing to do it, rain or shine. I couldn't get enough. Even the way she smelled was enlightening. It was a stench that did not exist in prison.

"It's time to go, Dave. I had a really nice morning," she said with a smile.

"I'll call you tonight," I promised.

She stood to her feet. I looked up at her, she gazed down at me. She took little, gentle steps closer to where I sat. Officer Terry had his eyes on her, ready to shout. "They don't like it when people get close," I whispered. She just smiled. It was a warm smile that I knew I'd remember for the rest of my days. The lightbulb on the ceiling was directly behind her head and cast a white glow around the perimeter of her face. She looked angelic, and then she kissed me. "Hey, cut that out!" Terry yelled out as he held his baton high.

"All right, all right!" she yelled right back.

She turned to me and smiled yet again. Then, she strutted away with the company of a guard. I watched every step she took until she left my sight. I sat in that metallic chair with feelings of euphoria rushing through me. Everyone else's goodbyes were white noise. I felt like I did when I was a teenage boy. It was always those kinds of things that kept your hopes up. I needed a lifeline and I had found one. I knew I had to speak with Earl eventually. I had to understand what it was truly going to take to get myself out of that place, but it would take some time to build the courage to be different.

Trouble in Block One

Earl's office was tucked away in the corner of Block 1. After a couple months, it was finally time I saw him. Parole was approaching within the year, and I needed to be ready. I had Officer Terry lead me to the office. He seemed a little on edge that day. He usually had a word or two of 'wisdom' to share but he was quiet. The sound of his tapping footsteps against the metal-grated walkway echoed. We strolled along the outside of jail cells filled with all sorts of people. Blacks, whites, Mexicans, Natives, Asians... They were all there, and just about every one of them looked at me as I passed. They knew I was going to see Earl.

"Yo Dave!" JC's voice sang through the block.

I twisted my head and saw JC sticking his arm out from his cell on the second floor. He was smiling. "Dave, up here," he screamed. The kid was an idiot. The other inmates in here wanted to kill him. I could tell instantly. I didn't respond verbally and presented him with a gentle nod. As I walked a few yards forward, I felt a sudden chill rush up my spine. Two pairs of eyes sat glowing in a dark cell that was filled with shadows. They blinked from within the blackness. The air suddenly grew colder. There was only one man that it could have been.

Terry led me right to Earl's door and he knocked. A warm sigh exhaled from his nostrils and he put his hands on his hips. "What a fucking day," he mumbled. I could hear Earl's footsteps. He was approaching the door, and through the hazy pane of glass at eye level, I could see the silhouette of the man. The shadow of his arm reached for the knob and the door swung right open to reveal a small office with a red couch and a printer, a wall with a degree and some personal photos hanging from it, and a desk with a computer. In the backdrop, there was a large window that looked right out to the highway that ran by the institution.

"Come on in," Earl uttered with a friendly gesture of his hand.

"Thanks, Terry," I said before entering.

The door slammed behind me. Earl whisked around me and sat right behind the desk and typed casually on the keyboard. "You are... David Spivey," he mumbled. "Yeah," I responded. The couch was soft and I sunk into it as I sat down. I exhaled and felt my muscles relax. The echo of fingertips slapping the tops of keys was calming. I closed my eyes for a brief moment.

"What the hell do you think you are doing, son?" Earl yelled out.

I snapped myself upright and coughed the phlegm from my throat. "Sorry," I mumbled. Earl sighed and shook his head, then he forcefully slammed down on top of the 'enter' button on the keyboard. "I got you," he said as he stood to his feet and approached the printer in the corner of the office. The machine whirred as pages started to flutter out. Earl stood by and waited for every last piece of paper to come out. The lights on the printer faded and the whirring noise halted. Earl picked up the stack and neatly organized it by tapping the bundle against the table. He leaned against his desk and crossed his legs. I sat on the couch upright. The shifting noise of paper filled the air as he flicked through my file.

"Oh, I see you, gangster," Earl said as read through the pages.

I gulped. I didn't know what to say. I said nothing. Earl's face was expressionless until he lifted his head to make a sly comment every other page. He mumbled things like; "Badass", "rockstar", and "legend." I didn't understand. He was mocking me with his tone and body language, commenting on every little part of my recorded life. He even went back through juvie and criticized me for being an aggressor at such a young age, fighting dudes older than me without fear. He finally set the bundle down and he crossed his arms.

"I thought you were supposed to help me, not make me feel bad," I stated.

"I made you feel bad?" he responded.

"You're making fun of me, man. If I knew it was going to be like this I never would have come."

"If you can't handle that, how are you supposed to deal with what they're gonna' say to you during your parole hearing?"

The words were lost within me. I didn't even bother opening my mouth. My lips were stapled together. I sat in the warmth of the office totally upright and still. He was right. "What're they going to say in my parole hearing?" I asked. A smile struck Earl's face and he pushed himself off his desk. He put his hands on his hips and gazed down at me.

"They're first going to speak about the facts. You're a cold-blooded murderer. You're a gangster. You've been around stabbings and race riots throughout your entire incarceration," he said as he paced around the room. "Then, they're going to start talking about the subjective things. You don't have a single dash on your record while you've been in prison, and they'll wonder why and make assumptions. They'll say that you could be paying off guards. They'll talk about the fact that you could be dealing drugs and maybe even killing people in here and getting away with it. They will immediately assume the worst, because they have seen you at your worst, and your worst is killing people," he followed passionately.

"So, this is a waste of time, huh?" I said with a shrug in my shoulder.

"It's only a waste if you think it is," Earl responded as he sat at his desk.

"Well, you're telling me that during my parole hearing, I'm going to get scolded for an hour before being sent right back to my cell."

"I didn't say that, did I?"

The air was silent but cool as a thin stream of cold air ran through the room. The flow was exerted from the AC unit high up on the wall in the corner of the space. It was nice. My cell was often muggy. Romeo spent a lot of time there so the stench of the place was naturally accustomed to his organic smell. I thought it was nasty and I placed fresheners next to my bed whenever I could get them shipped in.

"What my job is, Dave, is to make sure you understand yourself and what you're capable of. Now, I look through your file and I see a man who is lucky," Earl exclaimed.

"Lucky?" I responded with a chuckle.

"Do you know how many guys come into my office with the purest of intentions? Most. They come in here and they talk and they learn about themselves so they can prove to the parole board that they're rehabilitated... But then they go back to their cells, to the yard...

They blow it. Their loyalty drags them into situations that regular people don't understand. To you, it's protecting your brother from rivals, and you do it because you know they'd do the same for you. To them? It's primal violence. It's unacceptable."

The tattoos on Earl's arms and neck told a story. I was drawn to them. I had seen them many times before. We didn't roll from the same neighborhood, and we wouldn't have been allies back in the day, but I recognized his loyalties and where they lay. "I sat where you did once and I was told the same thing. Now, I'm on the other side, and I know what my mentor was feeling," he said. A sensation of reflection ripped right through me. It rattled me from the inside out and even my bones and muscles felt weak.

"A lot of you guys remind me of the man I once was. A younger version of me, one who sat in that chair you're in right now... I'm going to help you, Dave. We'll meet three times a week, and we'll discuss your mindset shift. But, starting right now, I want you to be conscious of your actions and environment. I want you to see yourself from the perspective of a civilian, who at their worst, might get a parking ticket. Do you understand me?" Earl stated passionately.

"Yes sir," I responded.

The walls of the prison felt like they were closing in on me after that. Everything felt fragile, especially life. I returned to my cell to see Romeo kicked back and watching Pimp My Ride. He was laughing his ass off. "No Family Feud?" I asked. Romeo shook his head. "Ain't on for another hour," he stated. I lay in my bed and removed the cell phone from under my pillow. I texted Nadine and told her about my morning with Earl. She was proud of me for putting myself first.

I hadn't told anyone, but I planned to propose to Nadine at her next visit. I didn't have a ring or anything like that, but I knew I loved her and I wanted to make sure she was mine when I stepped foot outside those walls. I had a vision of seeing her in a flowing white dress, standing by her car as I walked toward her, a free man. In my dream, my arms were wide and when I kissed her, I woke up. Waiting was frustrating, but I knew it would be worth it.

The tapping sound of footsteps on the grated metal walkway echoed in the air. I could tell it was Officer Terry. The beat of his step had become instantly recognizable. He walked to the door of our cell and immediately stuck his key in and swung it open. He was panicking. Sweat perspired on his forehead. He even dropped his keys in the middle of our room. "You're one clumsy motherfucker," Romeo mumbled as he watched TV.

"We need to talk, Romeo," he begged.

"About what?" Romeo responded.

"You know that shipment I told you was coming in today?"

"Yeah."

"It got held up. I think it's being taken all the way to the top," Terry said with a shake in his voice.

Romeo switched off the TV. He stood to his feet and squared up to Terry with a tilt in his neck. "What are you telling me, Terry?" he said. Terry's lips quivered and he nervously tapped his fingers against the butt of his baton. Romeo quickly grew impatient and pushed him against the bars of the cell. "What the fuck are you saying, Terry?" he yelled. Terry closed his eyes and shook in place.

"They know, man. They know I'm bringing drugs in here," he said with a stutter.

"Do they know who you're bringing drugs in for?" Romeo asked.

"No, no, they don't know. They found the package, and, and, I'm fucked, Romeo," Terry said with a struggle before closing his mouth.

Romeo took a deep breath, then he let go of Terry and turned to face me. "What do I do, Dave?" he asked. Romeo shot his gaze at me with a look of desperation painted across his face. Romeo grilled me with his eyes. A feeling of loom washed over me. That was the exact thing Earl was warning me about, but I couldn't express my true intentions. Loyalty came first, and I had to be smart.

"Are you sure they know it's you?" I asked Terry.

"I'm not sure, but, but, the other CO's... They know that I'm not like them. Especially that fucker Bailey," he responded.

"Okay, you've got plausible deniability, so deny. Don't break, don't even think about breaking. It will eventually blow over," I said.

The bells of the block buzzed and the noise it echoed was loud and sharp. Terry's eyes watered and his hands shook. It was yard time, and Terry had to step out of our room alongside us and direct us toward the door to the yard as he rounded up the other inmates. He just stood there as the buzzing rang loud. He didn't want to leave. "We gotta go, Terry," I reminded him. Terry nodded and opened the cell door for us.

Romeo and I were first in line to the yard. I could tell he was thinking deeply. He stared directly forward with a blank expression. Terry had rounded up all of the inmates and he opened the door to the yard. We all shared a silent exchange before stepping out into the light of day. The yard was completely empty. We were the first block to be let go, so Romeo and I strolled toward our usual spot in the center of the space.

"Do you think we can trust Terry?" Romeo whispered.

I stopped in my tracks. Romeo did the same and turned to me. "We?" I asked. "I'm not involved in your racket, motherfucker," I followed. Romeo exhaled and looked up to the blisteringly hot sun that cast white rays down onto us. He closed his eyes, deep in thought. "I thought we were boys, man," he said. Then, he opened his eyes once more and stared right into my soul. "I gave you a phone and everything. You wouldn't even be able to talk to that chick Nadine if it weren't for me," he followed. Romeo was right, but so was I. It was a fine line to walk, and I realized that I needed to navigate this situation smarter.

"You're right, man. I'm sorry. I think we should wait and see what happens. We don't know if Terry knows the whole story," I said.

"Yeah, that's smart," Romeo responded with a gentle nod.

"But you gotta lay low for a little while. Don't give the guards no reason to come snooping around our cell. Got that?"

"Only for a little while. Terry knows that if he does snitch, his family is going to get it. He knows that fully."

We stood in the center of the yard and watched as inmates began flooding into it from all of the cell blocks. The last doors to open were from cell block one. It was taking much longer than usual. "There must have been a riot," Romeo uttered. When a riot broke out in a block, they had no choice but to lock the whole thing down until the violence settled. If that was the case, then we weren't seeing our brothers that day.

A loud buzz rang and echoed into the air. The double doors to cell block one opened and out came flooding dozens of inmates. At the very back of the group, JC walked slowly toward us with wide eyes. Romeo perked up. "JC?" He could see something was off. JC stared into nothingness. He stumbled over an indent in the ground every other step. When he finally approached us, his cheeks trembled and Romeo placed both of his hands on his shoulders.

"You good, man?"

"Nah man... Nah, I'm not fucking good," he responded as he swatted Romeo's hands away.

"What the fuck is your problem?" Romeo yelled.

JC sat on his ass in the dirt. I scanned my surroundings and every pocket of inmates was whispering and turning to face us. Romeo hunkered down to JC. "What's good, man? Are you all right?" He asked. JC swelled up with tears. His breaths were short and sharp. He couldn't stay still. Romeo pushed JC into the dirt out of frustration. "Pipe the fuck up, rogue," he yelled. "Puma fuckin' raped me, man. He fuckin' raped me," JC said as tears rolled down his shaking cheeks.

Romeo's eyes widened. My heart stopped beating for a moment. I could feel a single bullet of sweat roll from the top of my neck and all the way down my spine to the crack in my ass. The air was still and silent and every pair of eyes watched as Romeo lifted JC to his feet and wrapped him in a hug. "What the fuck are you all motherfuckers looking at? I'll kill every fucking one of you. Turn yo' asses around," Romeo screamed out to the yard. I could see Bailey on the perimeter. She wore her reflective shades as usual but you just knew she was staring along with everyone else.

JC cried and cried and Romeo held him tighter and tighter. The rest of us didn't know what to do. We just stood there. Nobody turned away. It was the most action anybody got for a while. An inmate was raped. It never happened, until it did. The aftermath was shocking. The tremors exerted by JC's twitching muscles beat loudly. You could feel it at your own feet when the ground shook.

"Come on, JC. Get up. People are watching. Get up," Romeo whispered.

JC was helped to his feet and he leaned on Romeo. The rest of us circled him and blocked him off from the rest of the yard. Romeo's face was becoming purple with rage. His eyes were wide and unforgiving. "As soon as Puma gets out of the box, I want all you motherfuckers to be ready," he demanded. The sweat rolling down my back grew thicker and the slide of each bullet lasted longer. I could really feel the sun's heat and the burning gaze of the guards from behind me. To turn was treason, and the gang needed to be together now more than it ever had. That was my problem. Whenever Puma was going to step foot in that yard again, everything would change for that group of people. Loyalty was most important. We demanded that of each other. I dreaded that day right from that moment. I could hear Earl's words of advice spinning around inside my brain. Those were the words that were going to make me a free man, but they were also the ones that could make me a dead man.

A Nightmare in Inglewood

Wind rushes behind my ears as I pop the hood of my convertible. The sun beats warm rays down on my head. I wear sunglasses and there is ice on my wrist. Officer Bailey watches me from the gates of the prison. Her shades cover her eyes and expression. I see myself in the reflection, and I see a free man. Dust kicks up behind my car as I rev the engine and the wheels spin. The convertible dashes forward and leaves a cloud of smoke behind me that lingers in the air for a moment until it dissipates and the prison has vanished from the picture.

The dotted yellow lines on the highway come rushing at the front of my car as if I were a spaceship flying through stars at hyperspeed. The patchy hills and mountains that separate LA from the desert are high and the roads are winding. I twist and turn the wheel every other moment. There are no other cars. It is just me, and I'm going fast. The wheels spin as the vehicle climbs higher and higher, and when I reach the top, I see the city of Los Angeles shimmering in the grand distance. I slam my foot atop the brakes and the car skids forward. Steam rushes up the sides of the vehicle and blocks my vision for just a moment until the view comes back to me.

I pop the door open and I walk to the edge of the winding road. The fall is hundreds of feet to a rocky demise below. I gaze out at the town I love. The houses and high-rises span for miles. There is life out there. Nadine is out there. I have to get to her. My cheeks flap in the wind as I put my foot all the way down on the gas and accelerate down the mountain. Red-roof houses come into sight and I whizz along the highway through coming and going neighborhoods.

I swerve across three lanes. My tires screech. I scan my surroundings. I'm the only car out here, still. I've never seen that before. The air is warm and the sun is up. It's midday. It's a ghost town all the way to my exit, and then I see one car. It's parked at a red light just off the highway. The windows are tinted black. The tires are huge and within them are solid gold rims that sparkle in the sunlight. I halt alongside it and lean over. "Nice car, bro," I say with a smile on my face. It looks like a Mustang of some kind, but souped up and all-black. Steam surrounds its wheels and rolls along the pavement below like waves. Its engine revs and before the light even turns green it is gone from my sight and hundreds of yards ahead with a trail of dark smoke behind it. Nadine lives close by. I remember her address from the letters she sends me every once in a while. The houses in this neighborhood are brown and attached to one another. They have metal fences surrounding them. The front yards are filled with random shit like old shopping carts and broken children's toys. A thin layer of red paints the sky right above the horizon and the further I lean my head back the softer the hue gets until the atmosphere projects a purple and blue shimmer by the glowing ember sun. It's other-worldly and makes life below feel confused as a sudden rush of cold air blows by my feet and tussles my pants.

The car slows to a dribble as I squint my eyes to look at each house number. Nadine lives at number 15, and right now we're counting back from thirty. Each house is darker than the next, and the sunlight is dimming. The once-blistering celestial is now shadowed by a blue reflection that swallows the sky of its golden ember light. I stop outside her home. There is a red door in the dead center of the structure and two square windows on either side. The building blocks are popcorned. I step out of my rumbling vehicle and feel another rush of cool air blow right by me. I even catch the sight of hot steam rising from my exhale. The keys jingle in the ignition as the car purrs. I leave them there and take gentle steps toward my love's home. My heart beats a million miles per hour. Sweat forms on my fingertips and I rub them together nervously.

"Nadine, baby. I'm here," I whisper to myself as I walk toward the red door.

I close my hand to a fist and pound against the wood. Silence. The air is still and grows colder with every passing second. I rub my arms together. "Nadine, baby!" I yell. There's no response. I scan my surroundings and the entire neighborhood is silent and is actively being drained of its color in favor of a chilling blue hue.

A crash of pots and pans echoes from inside the house. I whip my head around and shimmy toward the window. I peer inside and see the living room. There is a dark yellow carpet and brown, leather furniture filling the space. A TV plays Family Feud with extreme brightness that creates a direct line of artificial light which particles of dust float inside and flutter to the ground. "Nadine?" I yell out. Nothing. I feel the gentle sensation of fluttering raindrops hitting against my skin. I lean back and above me, the gray clouds roll in like waves. Brief flashes of light spark within the darkness and reveal the skeleton of the altostratus. It looks like zebra stripes in the sky, with darkness in one row, and light in the next as the series repeats itself as far as my eyes can see. The wind picks up and rustles the shirt that I wear. The material flaps against my body and I struggle to stay balanced in one spot.

I walk around the perimeter of the home and I see that the back door is open. I stroll under the doorway with caution. "Nadine?" I yell out once more. The kitchen is uprooted and destroyed. There are appliances smashed to pieces, and on the stovetop, a pot of bubbling black liquid boils like hot tar. A stench of death rolls through. It shoots into my nostrils and my eyes widen with a burn. The tiles are chipped at my feet and food is strewn across the space. On the table there is a pistol. Its butt hangs over the edge and the barrel rests atop the wood. I take deep breaths as I lift it into my shaking hand. There are six bullets inside and I can smell the gunpowder exerting from the weapon.

A thump rumbles from a room at the end of the hallway. I approach the source of the sound. The wind and rain outside thrashes against the roof. It shakes the house. The walls creak and cracks spray along the inner foundation. Chips of paint and wood fall to the carpet below and dust sprinkles through the muggy air of the home. This place is going to fall. "Nadine!" I yell and yell.

There are four doors in the hallway. I rip the first one open and my heart freezes. The red-eyed silhouette of the creature that haunts my dreams sits tied up to an electric chair. Wires run around its undefined features and its piercing eyes stare into my soul. An ominous track of a single line of deep base hums. The rest of the room consists of a gray stone and is completely empty and lifeless. I stand in the ajar doorway with paralyzed muscles, when suddenly the bulb that hangs over the chair explodes into orange embers that flutter down onto the silhouette as the electricity pumps through the wires and burns the creature. Sizzling smoke rises into the air as the bloodshot red eyes keep their gaze on me. I turn and slam the door behind me. The house rumbles once again and dust falls from the ceiling. I lean against the wall with sharp and stinging breaths.

I rip door number two open and find a single, small child playing with toys in the middle of an empty room. It looks just like me. He pushes a train into an action figure and does not lift his head to acknowledge my existence. It is me. The words hang in my mouth. What should I say? Nothing. I'll say nothing. I close door number two. The air grows cold as I walk to door number three. I keep the child off my mind and focus on my mission to grab my love and leave this place once and for all.

A disgusting odor slinks beneath the crack of door number three. I pinch my nose and use my gun-wielding hand to push the door open. I close my eyes and take a deep breath, then I step into the space and gasp upon viewing the massacre. There are bodies stacked on top of bodies. There must be a dozen, and they're all young men. They're dudes like me, who dress like me and have tattoos like me. I take a step forward and hunker down to inspect further when my eyes shoot wide open and I gasp and fall onto my back. I kick myself away. The faces of these men are the same as mine. They are all me. All me when I was seventeen years old and gang banging. I turn away and slam the door shut behind me. I shake in my spot with my gun down by my side. I don't want to be in this house anymore. My body repels it.

A scream pierces my eardrums and I fall to my knees. My feet are too sensitive to walk on and I lie flat on the dirty carpet. I breathe heavily with sharp and short breaths as I try to push myself up but I do not have the strength. My eyes grow watery and they sting with the odor of death that lingers around the shaking house. Flashes of lightning fill the hallway through the windows every other moment and following is a rumble of thunderous applause. I'm afraid, but I can't give up. I yell with a nasty groan as I push myself to my feet and limp forward. Shadows dance across my face with every lightning strike and I grind my teeth down with every step. Door number four has a red light that shines through its cracks. The glow intensifies and retracts every other moment, like a lighthouse beacon spinning on a foggy night. My heart thumps against my chest. I have to see what's behind that door. "Nadine baby, just open the door and show me you're okay," I say with a croak in my voice. I can only hear the rumbling and shaking of the walls. Then, the cold returns. It breaks its way into the home and slithers along the walls until it reaches the hallway.

The air that flows through my lungs is chilling and I can feel the water within me freeze and halt the movement of my blood and fluids. I'm stiff and my skin turns blue. It starts at my fingertips and works its way up my arm. I struggle to close my hand to a fist. As I knock against the door, my bones suddenly creak and smash into thousands of tiny shards of ice. I scream at the top of my lungs and lift my handless arm to my eye level. The broken and shredded tip of my wrist squirts blood but after a moment it freezes into red icicles that snap and fall to the carpet below.

The chill shifts along my chest and torso and I feel my neck grow tighter and less mobile. It's now or never. I take one step back and crash through the door with all of the weight in my body. I land atop the wood and groan with the pain of the blow. My head is forced to stare at the door but I can hear the rumbling of deep voices and the squealing of a bed's springs and coils. My neck shakes as I try my utmost to lift it up. The freeze moves through my body and turns me to stone. My eyesight just about adjusts before movement becomes impossible and my vision is directed at the foot of a shaking bed. "Nadine," my quivering lips tremble. I can hear her. She's groaning.

I feel the ice freezing my blood. It's heading right towards my heart. Function is limited, and I fear that my next breath will be my last. The bed stops shaking. My eyes lift as high as they can go, but it's not enough to truly see. A pair of hairy black feet thump against the carpet before me. The toenails are yellow and strands of dust and cotton hide between the toes. "She ain't your girl anymore," the voice rumbles deeply. The house shakes. I close my eyes. Dark and ominous laughter echoes. "Go back to where you belong," the voice follows.

The tormenting storm rips the house apart and the walls and furniture are sucked up into the gray clouds above. The swirling rain and lightning thrash and flash around me as I lie frozen on the dark yellow carpet. The tears in my ears are preserved and refuse to drip into reality. My last breath is a cold and isolating one. I feel like a fucking fool.

Going All In

My dreams had been reminding me that I was a killer and I was nothing else. The image of a flashing, firing gun lit up my mind constantly. I could always hear the booming sound that followed. I could feel the bullet ripping through my skin and into my organs. Sweat ran down my forehead. I wiped it away with the sleeve of my orange overalls. Earl sat before me with his arms crossed. I stood in front of him. "Put your arms behind your back," he said. I followed his order. There was a strain in my neck as I lifted my chin up. I inhaled through my nostrils and relaxed my shoulders. "Ready?" I asked. Earl nodded silently. He picked up a pen and held it to a notepad that rested atop his knee.

"Why do you think you're deserving of parole after thirteen years, Mr. Spivey?" Earl asked.

"I know what I did was an atrocity against humanity. I hunted people down for sport. I've had nightmares every night because of it for the last thirteen years. I came into prison as a teenage boy, and I was not terrified. I was egotistical. I had a record in juvie and a reputation on the streets. Nobody messed with me and I liked it that way. Over time, I started to think more about who I was and what I had done. I watched as other inmates got in trouble for doing the same things I was doing. It was like looking in a mirror and realizing that I was lucky to still have an opportunity to prove to you that I can reform myself. After doing some time up north, I transferred to multiple different institutions with the sole intention of keeping a low profile and finding an environment that would help me grow in body and spirit. You now see me at year thirteen, and I want you to know that I have done everything in my power to change. I'm deeply sorry for what I did and I will never be able to bring back the life of the boy I killed, but I can instill positive values into young men who are on course to follow the same track that I did."

"Nope," Earl said casually.

"What do you mean 'nope'?"

"A piece of your past still thrives inside you. I can feel it, and so will the board. You're still a gangster, Spivey," Earl said as he closed the notepad over.

Earl arose from his seat and poured himself a glass of water. I sat in silence thinking about what I had done wrong. Everything I said was the truth. I was distancing myself from criminal activity as much as I could. Well, everything except for the cell phone. I needed that. "I don't understand," I stated. Earl sipped from his water and stared at me while he did it. He wanted me to marinate in thought. Then, he set his glass down and sighed a satisfactory sigh.

"A couple of the guards have been saying that your cellmate is a key player in the drug scene here. There are rumors he's using Officer Terry to bring the narcotics in. Is that true?"

"I don't know," I responded.

"Loyalty is instilled in us where we're from, Dave. Without it, you're a dead man. These people on the parole board? They don't all get it. They want to see will and intention, not isolation and excuses."

"What more can I do?"

"You can do more, pal. Trust me..."

I did have an idea. It was something that had been on my mind since I came to that prison. I didn't know how it could be achieved, but if it was going to help me get out of that place, I would make it work. "I was thinking about setting up a non-profit. I want to call it 'WARM', which would stand for 'We Are More'," I exclaimed. Earl nodded his head and puckered his lips with his arms crossed. "And?" He asked.

"And, it'll be for low-lives. The foundation will spread positivity through bad neighborhoods, where people like me and you came from," I said.

"They already got stuff like that, Dave," Earl said with a sigh.

"No, they don't. See, WARM is about positivity in name. We're going to strive to remove labels in the neighborhood so everyone can feel welcome... How many times have you heard somebody call a dude a crackhead?"

"A lot of times."

"How do you think it makes them feel?"

"Never thought about it."

"Most people don't, but WARM will try to shed light. We'll spread positivity through low-economic neighborhoods and inspire people to simply be a member of their community and not a labeled outcast. You feel me?"

Earl leaned back silently with his arms crossed. His lips were sealed and his gaze fell upon me with half-opened eyes. "Time's up, Dave," Earl said as he walked toward me and patted me on the shoulder. I rose to my feet and looked him in the eye. "Good luck today, by the way," he followed with a devilish smile. I nodded my head and thanked him.

That day was one of the biggest days of my life. I had a video visit with Nadine. I had a plan and I had been waiting to execute on it since I first spoke to her. I was freshly showered and I made sure I got as much sleep as I possibly could, even though that was always going to be minimal. Nerves ran through me but I didn't care. I was excited to see her face, even if it was behind a computer screen.

I waited by the cream-colored door to the video visitation room. Every doorway looked the same as the next all the way down the hallway. Footsteps tapped on the tiled floor. The noise echoed from behind me and grew louder with every second. "Mr. Spivey," a female voice rang. I turned and saw Officer Bailey approach me and scan me from head to toe. "Hello Officer," I said. She looked at the door to the video visitation room. The light above it was red. "They've got two more minutes, and then it's your turn," she said. "Thank you, officer," I responded.

"You're one of Earl's students, right?" she asked.

"Yes ma'am."

"He's mentioned you on several occasions," she said.

"He's a good man," I responded.

The red light above the door switched to a green and a soft buzz echoed. The entryway opened and out came a dude named Dan. We called him 'Dan the Man' because he was an artist who sold his prison paintings to rich people on the outside. He lived like a king in that institution, and even if he was on the outside, he'd still be considered a wealthy man. The art he created told the story of what we were all living, and I guess some dudes just *vibed* with it enough to pay thousands of dollars for it.

"What's good, Spivey?" he mumbled to me.

"I'm about to see my girl," I responded.

Dan smiled a Hollywood smile and lifted his chin. "Spivey, you're in. Dan, you're walking with me," Bailey said as she grabbed Dan's shoulder. They walked down the hallway in silence. Bailey looked over her shoulder a couple times to get a glimpse of me. I stepped into the visitation room. The walls were egg-shell white and there was one old box computer at a wooden desk. A video camera sat atop the machine and aimed at the crooked wooden chair opposite it. The screen was black. I gently rubbed my hand around the entire thing to find the 'on' button. It was taking me much longer than it should have.

"How the fuck do I work this thing?" I whispered to myself.

Nadine's face suddenly flashed on the screen. She was smiling. I sat back in my chair and threw my hands behind my head. "Your biceps are looking bigger," she said. I flexed for her and gave her a show. She was laughing and giggling. The background in her video was her local library. People were walking around with books and DVDs in their hands. She was in some sort of glass booth.

"I missed you," she said with the tilt of her neck.

"Me too," I responded.

"Your parole hearing is coming up. How are you feeling about it?" she asked.

"I feel good, baby."

She shifted uncomfortably in her chair. I could tell she wasn't as positive about it as I was. I understood. There was a lot of uncertainty that came with parole. Every member of the board had to be in agreement. I even had to convince the mother of the boy I killed that I was safe for release. It was not an easy feat. It required honesty, trust, and change. Nadine wasn't seeing me every day, so she couldn't have noticed the sweat equity invested in bettering myself. All she knew was what I told her over the phone.

"You gonna' pick me up when I get out or what?" I asked with a smile.

"Flowing white dress, right?" she responded.

I had to ask the question right then and there. Her beauty had drawn me in completely and I thought that it was 'now or never'. I got down on one knee and everything. Her eyes popped and her jaw dropped. She placed her open palms on her cheeks. "Are you serious, Dave?" she squealed. "Yeah baby," I responded. She started to cry. She couldn't speak at all. I waited a good ten seconds for an answer. It was the longest stretch of time I had ever felt.

"Yes, Dave. Of course baby," she managed to say through the sniffles.

That was a peak moment in my life. I left the video visitation room with a fat smile on my face and a fiancee by my side. Somebody had shown that they loved me and committed to a future that may not have even existed. I was grateful for that. Officer Bailey led me back to my cell and I didn't say a damn word. I just hazily looked forward with a glimmer in my vision. She didn't like it very much, especially when she asked me questions that went unanswered.

"All right, Dave."

Bailey stopped and dragged me in front of her. My dreamlike vision returned to reality and I could see the frustration on her face. "I know about Officer Terry. We have enough evidence to throw him behind bars along with you guys," she stated. The air stood still. All I could hear was the water rushing through the pipes that were hidden by the walls. "I don't know what you're talking about," I responded. She smiled. That woman was sharp and she knew I was bullshit. I could tell she was hot on his trail and close to putting her claws in him. She was queen cat around that place.

"Earl says there's a good chance you could get parole in the near future. Is that right?" she asked.

"Yeah," I responded.

"You've been working hard to improve. I've noticed that. A lot of the guards have, too. It'd be a shame if none of them vouched for you because of your loyal associations, now wouldn't it..." she followed.

"Why are you saying these things?"

"You know why. Come on," she said as she continued walking.

Bailey and I reached my cell. We could see Romeo inside watching TV with his legs kicked back and a bag of chips in his hands. He didn't bother turning to acknowledge us. "All right, in you go, Dave," Bailey said as she swung the door open and gestured for me to enter. I looked at her as she gently nodded to me and then went on her way. Her footsteps echoed until they didn't, then I swung myself around to gaze at Romeo. "What're you watching? I asked. "Cops," he responded as he threw a handful of chips into his mouth.

I lay back on my bed and looked up at the ceiling. Nadine was on my mind. "Hey, wanna hear some good news?" Romeo asked. I sat up in my bed and looked at him. He turned off the TV and swung around to face me. He was smiling like the devil himself. His eyes were wide and filled with the illusion of a redeeming idea.

"What is it?"

"Puma is coming back to the main yard in three months. Terry told me," Romeo stated.

"No shit," I responded.

I didn't even have to ask. Romeo wanted Puma dead, and everyone knew it. I didn't care. My parole hearing was coming up and by the time 120 days rolled around, I would be gone, sitting on Nadine's couch with her head on my lap. I wouldn't be hunting another man down with a rusty knife through hordes of inmates on a hot day. I wouldn't be DP'd for it either. I'd be my own man with no connection to the past.

"We're gonna' take care of this motherfucker," Romeo said as he squeezed his fist tight.

"Damn right," I responded.

"I told Terry to sneak in some retractable knives."

"Romeo, man. Don't be dumb. You know Terry's on thin ice as it is," I reminded him.

"It's cool, Dave. Trust me... And, don't worry, I told him to bring one for you, too," he said.

The acid within my stomach bubbled fiercely. Gravity weighed heavily upon my head. I wanted to kill him on the spot. I really felt like I was going to. I had immediate thoughts of wrapping my hands around his neck and planting evidence to make it look like he asphyxiated himself for pleasure and died doing it. I was close until Officer Terry's keys came crashing to the grated metallic ground outside the cell. "You're one clumsy motherfucker, Terry," Romeo said with a chuckle. Terry came into our cell and nervously slipped the keys back into his pocket. He was visibly shaking. "You got the shipment?" Romeo asked. Terry nodded and removed a brown and thin but long bag of heroin from his back pocket and tossed it onto Romeo's lap. Terry looked at me with wide and terrified eyes. They were begging for help while his mouth stayed pinned shut.

"Where are the knives?" Romeo asked.

"Romeo, man. This has to be the last time we do this, okay? People are investigating me, man. It took all fucking day just to get the heroin in, so forget the knives!" Officer Terry exclaimed passionately.

"You didn't bring the knives?"

Romeo stood up from his chair and shifted toward Terry. Romeo's shadow engulfed him and Terry's eyes were glistening with tears. I stayed seated on my bed and watched as Terry's cheeks trembled. "Where are the knives that I gave you money for?" Romeo asked aggressively. Terry's hand shook as he slipped into his pocket and removed a crumbled, dirty fifty-dollar bill. Romeo slapped it out of his hand and then punched Terry in his left eye.

Terry stumbled back against the bars and Romeo came in with another blow to his face. Terry slid down the bars and on the way Romeo kicked him in the gut. Terry fell forward and landed with his face an inch from the ground. He was coughing viciously and crawling on his hands and knees. "What the fuck are you doing, kid?" I yelled as I jumped from my bed and pinned Romeo to the wall. He squirmed with the pressure of my grasp but I was stronger. "Get the fuck outta my way, Dave," he yelled.

Terry stumbled a couple times as he rose back to his feet. Blood seeped from a gash on his lip and dripped down onto his pants and shoes and stained them in blotches of dark red. "Get out of here, Terry. Tell them someone else did this," I said. Terry was speechless and shook even more violently. He left and completely forgot to close the cell door behind him. The echo of his trudging footsteps grew softer and softer as he shifted further away. I pulled myself away from Romeo and he immediately pushed me onto my bed.

"This is my business and I do things how I do them. You got that?" he yelled.

"Yeah," I responded.

Romeo shook his head and exhaled. He threw his hands on his hips. We existed in silence for just a moment, until Romeo switched the TV back on and sat back with his legs kicked up. What I had seen was not only violence against an officer but aggravation against a man. We are prideful creatures who do not forget, and I knew that at that moment, Terry was desperately thinking of a way to remove himself from the situation we all found ourselves in. He wanted Romeo dead more than anyone. I couldn't be dragged down with all of this.

"Yo' Romeo," a voice bellowed from outside the cell.

We both turned and saw Dan the Man standing in the opened doorway of our cell. "Dan, my brotha. What can I do for you?" Romeo said as he perked up. Dan entered. "Half an ounce," he casually responded. Romeo nodded and began emptying out heroin from the fresh bag and onto a scale that he hid underneath his chair. "So, you working on anything right now?" Romeo asked as he weighed the drugs. "Man, just shut the fuck up and give me shit," Dan responded while rolling his eyes. Romeo gulped and stayed quiet. He had no choice but to. Dan had the money to get anything done in prison. Anything. While Romeo tied up the baggie, Dan smiled at me. "How'd it go?" he asked. I gave him a thumbs up. I didn't want Romeo to know just yet. I didn't trust him with any piece of knowledge. "Here you go, brotha'," Romeo said as he handed Dan the bag of heroin. A fist bump and a wad of cash were exchanged between the two men and Dan closed the door behind him as he left our cell. It was silent once more and I decided to close my eyes and manifest my release. To do that, I would have to go over the words I would use during my hearing. I had to think about the tone in which I would speak and the emotions I would choose to express.

"What was Dan asking about?" Romeo piped up.

"What?"

"Dan asked you how something went. What was it?"

"It was nothing, man."

"You propose to Nadine or something?"

"No."

"Yeah, you did. You're always on that damn phone with her talking about the future and shit. This is a small cell, man, I hear you on that phone," he said with a smirk. "Just tell me I'm right," he followed.

"Yeah, but I ain't really engaged because I didn't have a ring. So, I guess you could say we just made a promise," I responded. "Now, shut the hell up and let me sleep," I followed.

"All right, loverboy. I just hope she keeps that promise," he said before turning up the volume higher on the TV.

I was laying on my shoulder and facing the wall. I could see my own silhouette from the artificial rays that were being cast from the TV. My eyes were open wide and my thoughts raced through me. I didn't think she would ever be unfaithful. She was my girl and she made that clear. My phone never stopped buzzing. I had no reason to suspect anything, and frankly, I didn't need to have any thoughts like that in my mind at that moment. I was going for parole in just a few weeks, and after thirteen years, I was ready. I felt rehabilitated and I wanted to have the opportunity to prove that to the board. I prepared for a battle and I came into that meeting with my shoulders high and my head held straight. I was clean and serious with every action I made and words I said. I kept Earl's advice close to my heart. It guided me through the torment of the words that were being flung at me from all angles. The two men and two women on the board were ruthless, but I stayed true to myself and I answered everything with dignity and honesty. They each berated me with their curiosities and carefully inspected my responses. Both of the mothers of my victims were there. My mind was focused on only one thing and I wanted my freedom. The idiocracy of Romeo and the gang in which I stood loyal was not going to drag me down into the fiery pits of a hellish existence.

The King of the Jungle

I was still a danger to society. That's what the board said about me. I understood, but I was disappointed. All four of their faces looked at me from the other side of a large wooden table in an eggshell white room. A woman sat in the corner typing everything I said into a laptop. The mothers of my victims sat on the edge and I could barely look at them. Those on the board read through my whole file while I sat there and stayed quiet. I spoke when I was given a chance to speak, and I listened when they had something to say. I did everything I could and they still failed me. I would not be legally allowed to have another parole date for another three years, but Earl showed me how to submit a petition to the board to advance my next parole date. I would find out shortly when that would be. I just couldn't believe that I had put so much thought and effort into bettering myself and nothing had come from it.

After word came through about the denial, I had Nadine visit me in person. She cried a lot. It was a major blow to our relationship. There was now an even more undefined future. She held on for me, still. She was strong. She even kissed me right on the lips in the visitation room again even though she knew she would get in trouble. I loved her. That was the worst week I had since my mother and brother died. I felt like a bum, a disappointment who deserved to be behind bars for the rest of his days. How could I argue? My victims' parents said so themselves. Their lives had been changed forever by me. I murdered one son and destroyed the life of another. "Thirteen years ain't long enough," the common statement was. I was now just like the other inmates. I was a criminal floating through the judicial system, and a wave of problems was coming right at me.

"Today is the day, Dave," Romeo said as he shook me awake one morning three months after my parole hearing.

I awoke with crusty eyes. I wasn't even dreaming anymore. I fell asleep at night and woke up in the morning. Nothing was going on. I was tempted to ask Romeo for some narcotics, but I held on for Nadine. I didn't want her to think that her husband-to-be was still a druggie. I promised her that I wasn't. Romeo paced around the room with excitement. He held a shiv in his hand. It didn't have a handle and the blade looked blunt. That thing would have hurt him more than anybody else.

"Is that what you're planning to use?"

"Yeah, why?"

"Just curious," I responded as I got out of bed.

The ground was cold to touch that morning. A tingle was sent along my toes, through my feet, and up my shins until I felt a shiver in my spine. The sensation of impending doom loomed over me like a rain cloud. I couldn't express it to anyone with my words. I had to live in it. Romeo didn't bother watching TV that morning. He walked back and forth and practiced slicing and stabbing motions.

"We're gonna' get him in the yard," he said to me.

"That ain't smart," I told him over and over.

He didn't listen. The yard was the only place where he could assert his dominance for the entire prison to see. He wanted to prove that he was king around that place and a king is also a showman. Puma had disrespected him and the gang in which we stood. He had a point to make. Everybody and their mother was expecting it.

The day started with breakfast in the cafeteria. There was a lot of chatter. It rang loud and echoed in the room. Folk were laughing and joking around with each other. My table was more serious. JC still quivered at the touch of another man. Romeo's eyes were fiery and unrelenting. He didn't blink. He just scanned the room and made eye contact with anyone who stared back. He held his spoon with a clenched fist. I couldn't bear it. The guards that patrolled the perimeters of the space had their gaze on us. We were the problem children, the ones who were at the highest risk of inciting a fight. I hated that I was associated with them and I detested the fact that it might have had a role in my denial of parole.

A whistle rang through the air. We all turned our heads. Earl stood by himself in a three-piece suit. He wiggled his index finger at me. "Go to Daddy," Romeo muttered. I sighed and rose to my feet. I didn't want to finish the food on my tray. It was bland oatmeal and grits. Disgusting. My feet felt like they had chains on them as I walked. The ground pulled me down and my shoulders were dropped low like the ears of a cowering dog.

"Good morning, David," Earl said to me.

"Mornin."

"I've got good news. The board has accepted your request for a parole hearing a little over a year from now."

Over a year. It seemed like a lifetime. I had come so close already and I felt like the carrot was being dangled before me. "Can I ask you something, Earl?"

"Sure," he responded.

I had to find the right words to express what was on my mind. I didn't want to appear ungrateful, but I also didn't want to chase a dream for the rest of my life.

"Will I ever get out of here?"

"That's for you to decide, son," Earl responded as he put his hand on my shoulder.

"I tried starting a non-profit. It didn't work because nobody wants to do business with a dude in jail. I tried separating myself from the gang, but my own cellie is a murderous whackjob. I studied, took classes, and I worked countless odd jobs for the prison. I feel like all of it has just gone unnoticed," I exclaimed.

"Well, that's because it has. Nobody cares about what an inmate does. They care about what you did, and you murdered somebody, Dave... What people want to see is not only remorse, but they want consistent action. You have to sweat to prove that you can be a member of society. Physically and psychologically. You keep working hard until your next hearing, and I promise you that the environment will be warmer."

Earl shook my hand in front of hundreds of inmates. I didn't care. I don't think anybody else did, really. We were all tough motherfuckers, but we were still people. We wanted to be free.

Nobody enjoyed being in prison, except for maybe Puma. I returned to the table and was met with instant criticism from Romeo.

"You a fool if you think they ever gonna' let you out of here," he said.

Silence was golden. I finished my meal and put my tray away. I wanted to get back to my cell as quickly as possible so I could call Nadine and tell her about the new parole date. She would only have to wait another year. It was doable, considering she had already spent so much of her time on me. Excitement bubbled within me for the first time in ages.

The second I returned to my cell I jumped onto my bed and ripped out the phone from beneath my pillow. Romeo sat on the edge of his bed and twirled the beat shank around his hand. I opened my phone and my perspiring fingers slammed atop the buttons in rapid succession. I held the device to my ear and shot up to my feet. I paced around the room as the dial tone echoed in my ear. My heart beat fast. The ground was chilled.

"Hey Dave," Nadine spoke through the speaker.

"Hey baby, how are you doing?" I asked.

"I'm good, Dave," she responded.

The tone of her voice was different. She sounded deflated and tired. "You sure you're okay?" I asked again. Silence. Static hung in the air for several moments. I could hear her gentle breaths through the speaker. I waited impatiently for an answer. "I got good news, girl," I told her. The silence remained.

"I got something to say, Dave," Nadine stated.

"What's up?"

Romeo turned to look at me. I kept my back to him and pinned the phone as tight as I could to my ear. I heard sniffling on the other line. Nadine struggled to get the words out of her mouth. "Just tell me what's up, baby," I said. Romeo smiled and leaned back, gazing up at the ceiling. My mind raced through hundreds of possibilities during that silence.

"I met another dude, Dave. I'm gonna marry him," she said.

"Another dude? What the fuck do you mean 'another dude'? We're engaged, Nadine."

"I know we are. I'm calling it off."

"I don't understand. I - I'm having another parole hearing in a year, that's all you gotta wait," I said desperately.

"You're not getting parole, Dave. I can't be married to a prisoner. I've got needs."

"You sound just like your bitch mother," I said angrily.

"Goodbye, Dave."

Just like that, everything driving me forward had disintegrated into nothingness. I remained a murderous convict, unable to show affection or to be loved. I sank onto my bunk and stared at the floor. Romeo laughed. "You gettin' cheated on, ain't you?" He said smugly. He was like a little chihuahua. All bark, no bite. I took a deep breath and composed myself, but the fucker just kept coming.

"Girl's gotta get dick, man," Romeo exclaimed.

I pounced on him like a lion and wrapped my hands around his neck. His eyes bulged and his skin turned slightly purple. Veins popped from my forearms and I squeezed tight. Romeo kicked and squirmed.

I could see the light slowly draining from him, and I realized how stupid I was. I ripped myself from him and stood tall over him.

"That was a fucking DP, motherfucker. I'm sick of you talking to me like you're a goddamn general. You're an idiot and you're gonna find yourself dead one day if you keep acting the way you do," I said firmly.

That was the first time I had seen Romeo quiver. He was silent and he nodded at me. There was a plot behind his eyes and I had a feeling that he was thinking of a way to get back at me. At that moment, I could not have cared less. I laid down onto my bunk and I stared at the ceiling. We both waited for that bell to buzz so we could step out into the yard. Then, I heard the sound of keys clattering against the metal-grated walkway outside my cell.

"What the fuck do you want, Terry?" Romeo said.

Terry stayed outside the cell. He picked up his keys calmly and slipped them back into his pocket. His cheeks spread as he plunged his face between two bars with a smile. Romeo perked up. He stood to his feet. "What the fuck are you smiling about?". Terry started laughing. He had a crazy look in his eyes.

"You're fucked, Romeo," he said.

"What did you do?" Romeo responded as he walked to the door to meet Terry head-on.

"I'd be expecting a little visit from Officer Bailey this evening."

"You motherfucker."

Romeo punched through the gaps in the bars but Terry jumped back. Romeo desperately tried to reach the shirt of the officer but Terry stood back smiling and laughing. Wrinkles riddled the inmate's face. He growled and swiped. "What the fuck did you do, Terry?"

"I snitched, you motherfucking asshole," he responded.

Romeo clenched his fists and pulled himself away from the bars and stood tall. His cheeks trembled fiercely. "Your family's dead, man. All it takes is one call," Romeo said.

"I got a deal for confessing, you fucking idiot. The jig is up... I guess all silver has to turn to gray at some point, right?"

Terry scoffed at Romeo and walked away. The sound of his footsteps echoed until they did not. Romeo stood there in silence. He breathed heavily through his nostrils. His shoulders rose and fell with every inhale and exhale. It was at that moment that I knew it was judgment day. The walls of that place were crumbling and I did not want to find myself in the wreckage. The silence lasted for a moment until the bell of the block buzzed and rang loud for everyone to hear. Romeo grabbed his shiv and slipped it into the pocket of his orange jumpsuit.

The light of the sun was blinding. Rays of white light shone down onto the yard as inmates spilled into it with loud chatter. I stood next to Romeo, JC, and the other silent members of our gang in the dead center of the space. Our eyes were scanning every face that passed. A cool breeze circumnavigated the yard and rustled the cuffs of our jumpsuits. The chill rushed up my legs.

"You better not bitch out, Spivey. Otherwise imma make sure you get DP'd, and imma' make sure your ex-girl gets DP'd, only a different kind of DP. You feel me?"

Being in a gang in prison had taught me a lot about myself. I was insanely loyal. I was so dedicated to my beliefs and brothers that I would have done anything for them even if I did not like them. It was a code I chose to live by and it was a trust that I had earned throughout my days as a gangster. I was ready for it to all be over. The fine line that I walked was thinning. Death seemed like the likeliest outcome.

Puma came walking out of a set of double doors. He was thin and malnourished. He had visibly aged. The hairs on his head were gray and so was his patchy beard. His arms were thin and lacked definition. He smoked a cigarillo and constantly licked his chapped lips after exhaling a cloud of dark smoke. Heads turned and watched as he sauntered by with a smirk. He was basking in the spotlight. Romeo scanned the perimeter and saw several guards eyeing him. Bailey was one of them and her hand was held down low by the trigger of her gun.

"When Puma gets close, we go at him. All of us," Romeo said as he looked at me specifically.

"The second we move those guards are firing rubber bullets," I piped up.

"We only need one hit. Aim for the neck," Romeo responded.

Everybody put their hands in their pockets and grabbed hold of their homemade weapons. I stayed calm. My breathing was consistent and precise. Puma was strolling closer and closer. He knew what he was doing. His gaze would flicker my way every other moment. Everybody knew what was about to happen. Romeo ground his teeth. The screech was loud. JC shook in place. His legs vibrated and his feet dug into the dirt below. He breathed long deep breaths through his nostrils.

Puma stopped and stood before the group of us. A slimy smile came across his beaten, scratched, and withered face. The dry skin jutting out from his lips had jabbed tips. He licked them with his blue tongue. "Sup' JC," he said. JC gulped. The muscles in his forearm tightened as his hand clenched onto the shiv in his pocket. Puma then moved his gaze to meet me. "Look at us, Spivey. We're the old guys now," he said.

Romeo stepped forward. He was no more than five feet from Puma. "I wanna watch you bleed, motherfucker," he said. The wind died to a lull. The sun's rays beat down hot onto our already weak bodies. The glisten in our eyes was gone and what remained was lifeless and black. There was one final exhale, and then chaos ensued.

Romeo ripped the shiv from his pocket and lunged at Puma. Officer Bailey immediately fired a shot into the air. "Everybody get on your fucking stomachs right now!" Dust kicked up into the sky and muddied my vision. Guys in my gang screamed and ran forward with knives. I looked around and other inmates of various segregation had already fallen flat onto the ground. It was just us, and we were in the spotlight. The yells and screams came from behind the wall of dusty smoke that hung in the air. I lifted my arm to better my vision and I stepped toward the brawl. Puma ripped a knife from one of us. He crouched low and waved the blade at Romeo and the boys. "Come on, Romeo," Puma taunted. Another dude pounced at the rapist and quickly suffered a perforated blow to his abdomen. He dropped his weapon to the ground and blood spilled all over the dirt. My breathing was fast and sharp. There were guards in full armor rushing toward us with guns aimed in our direction. In just a few moments, every single one of us would be given a one-way ticket to the hole.

I saw the rest of my life flash before my eyes. "David Spivey; Inmate, murderer, helpless." That's all I would ever be. The opportunity to get parole was a balloon that was quickly elevating out of my reach. I thought about how my mother would be so disappointed in me. Auntie Cheryl was shaking her head in the clouds. She had her arm around my little brother and she kept him warm. I couldn't disrespect them. My life was the only part of them that continued to exist and I'd be damned if I spent it incarcerated.

I dropped to the dusty ground and put my hands behind my head. I looked forward to the commotion. It was just Puma and Romeo, surrounded by a cloud of dusty smoke. They each held a knife and stepped from side to side like brawling crabs, waiting for the other to make a move. "I'm the fucking king of this jungle," Romeo yelled. Puma laughed. The guards were approaching as a unit.

The dust was dissipating before my eyes. The rest of my gang all lay on their stomachs, including JC. I looked into his eyes and they were filled with fear for the future. He gazed up like a lost puppy, watching as his leader swayed his dirty blade around. Puma dodged every swipe like a master, and in a swift blow, he tumbled to the ground and sliced his weapon across Romeo's calf. Romeo screamed and Puma jumped up behind him and held his knife to Romeo's throat. His Adam's apple scraped off the blade as he gulped. Puma leaned in close and licked his ear. Then, he whispered into it. I couldn't tell what was said, but Romeo's eyes shot wide open and before I could blink blood was splattered onto the dirt right before my face. Romeo lifted his hands to cover the neck wound but blood spilled through his fingers and ran down his arms and dripped to the dirt. The ground shook as Romeo fell to his knees and stared at me with his last ounce of life. His lips quivered before his eyes closed and he fell face-first into the dust. Puma stood tall, chest puffed out. He threw his hands into the air and let out a battle cry.

"*I'm* the king of this motherfuckin' jungle!"

Officer Bailey fired a rubber bullet into the rapist's chest and he fell to his knees laughing. She let a couple of the other guards pick him up and take him away while she pointed her gun at all of us gangsters who lay flat on our stomachs. I closed my eyes and took deep breaths. A shadow engulfed me. I looked up and Bailey stood over me with her weapon aimed right at my face. I hoped to God I wasn't getting sent to the hole. One dash on my record would have killed me. I prayed to mom. I asked her to help me as if I were just a young boy again.

"I saw the whole thing go down, Spivey. Get your ass back to your cell," she said before moving on to the other inmates.

I don't know why I was spared, but I was grateful. The other dudes in my gang were all thrown in the hole for months. They were made an example of. When they'd be released, I wondered if they'd come for me. After all, I retreated during a fight. I broke the code to protect my own interests. But, when those boys crept back into the yard, they left me alone. I didn't even see Puma again. I don't know where he went. He could have transferred institutions, or he could have been sent to protective custody for the rest of his life. It didn't matter to me. I was given a chance to work hard and in silence. I took advantage of the opportunities given to me every single day. Sweat rolled down my back from labor and crinkles formed on my brain from stressful thinking but I was improving. I was becoming the man that I wanted my mother to see me as, and I would not stop until I walked out the gates of that institution as a free man.

A Dream in Incarceration

Everything is dark. A pair of warm, soft hands touch my cheeks and an angelic voice tells me that she loves me. My shoulders weigh down gently as two yellow straps are thrown over me. I open my eyes to a gentle light. The laces on my shoes are tied like bunny ears, and a blue shirt covers my torso like a poncho. The air is warm and a familiar smell floats from the oven into my nostrils. The door is opened and steam exerts from the cooker and into the air. The heavenly odor washes over me and I close my eyes. The smell of a concoction of meat, potatoes, and cheese is almost hallucinating.

"David baby, it's time for school," the voice echoes.

I float through the air and land on the stoop of my home. The sky is blue and there is not a cloud to be seen. The sun casts an ember glow that rains rays down onto my freed skin. The grass in the yard is green and watered, and across the street, the neighbors wave. A yellow school bus pulls up outside of my house and parks by the curb. The door swings open and the driver gestures to me. I turn and look upwards. The angel of my life smiles down at me, then she kisses my forehead.

The bus doors close behind me. There are rows of empty seats. "Which one is mine?" I ask. "Whatever one you want," the driver responds. I stroll down the red aisle and slip into a yellow seat. I set my backpack down beside me and my legs dangle over the edge of the two-seater. My hands are placed on the rails of the chair before me. My head is turned to the streets we pass by. There are men, women, and children all walking along a clean sidewalk.

We stop outside of a three-story apartment building. The brown door entry sits above a row of steps that lead down to the sidewalk. It swings open and standing in the doorway is my friend Star. He wears a backward purple cap and he has his backpack thrown over one shoulder. "See ya', ma'," he yells before rushing onto the bus. Star sees me and sits next to me. We dap each other up. We have our own way of doing it. It starts with a regular high five, but then it evolves into something so much more. There's elbows, feet, and knuckles involved.

The bus continues to move. Star and I laugh uncontrollably and kick our legs about. Our heads turn to the front of the bus when we hear the doors open and Markus steps on. "What's up, guys!" His high-pitched voice squeals. He jumps along the aisle and slips into an open two-seater and kicks his legs out with a stretch. "What'd I miss?" He says with a smile on his face.

Steam blows out the exhaust as the bus whizzes through South Central neighborhoods. The buildings are pure and glowing with warm light. We stop outside of an Asian restaurant and out comes running Xing. His parents sprint out after him but he gets onto the bus just in time. "You're supposed to work today!" They yell. Xing pants with heavy breaths as he sits in the first row and bows his head. The driver puts his foot down on the accelerator and we spring forward quickly.

Xing is silent at the front of the bus. The rest of us joke around like it's our job. I laugh so hard that I kick the back of the seat in front of me and screws fall out onto the floor. "Hey, watch it!" The driver yells out.

"Sorry," I respond.

The wheels of the bus gradually slow down. We all pin our little heads to the glass window. There's a bus stop ahead and multiple children are standing by it. A gust of wind blows through the interior as the doors swing open. One by one, children spill into the vehicle. Philly enters wearing a wife-beater and no backpack. He holds his lunch box down by his side and goes all the way to the back of the bus. Eric steps on next. He's taller than the other kids. He wears Jordans and black basketball shorts. He looks cool as hell. He waits at the top step for Joe to come on, and when he does he trips on the stairs and falls at Eric's feet. Eric helps him up and they stroll down the aisle and sit a couple rows behind me. Chains is next, and he plays music loud from his phone and freestyles along with the beat. JC follows him. He's tiny, and he cowers away from eye contact. Eric gestures for the kid to come sit with him and Joe. JC slips in next to Eric and the three all make their introductions and start talking about basketball and baseball. Jamie gets on last, and he has no friends. He wears a large hood that covers the top half of his face. I don't know how he sees anything. He sits all the way down the back a row away from Chains.

"Everybody all good?" The driver yells out.

"Yes," a collective response booms through the vehicle.

The neighborhood homes start to vanish and the bus is on course for a glowing light in the distance. The rays shine through the windscreen and creep along every row of the bus. Light fills the interior and reveals the glowing particles of dust that hang in the air and float with the gentle wind that circumnavigates us. Laughter rings through the air and an intense sensation of warmth is wrapped around me like a motherly blanket. The ember sun is bright and welcoming. I take a calming breath and exhale with a gentle sigh. The silhouette of Auntie Cheryl's house shimmers in the distance. A touch of love strikes me. I'm ready.

I am David Spivey

The feeling of being watched was intense. There were six eyes in heaven that looked down on me. It was the morning of my second parole hearing. I sat alone in my cell while my cellie ate breakfast in the cafeteria. The clock next to my bed ticked loudly. It consumed the silence in the room. I had become used to my surroundings. That was home to me. I knew every single inch of the space. There was a clump of dust in the corner that never moved. A drip that dropped from the ceiling would make a sound once every two and a half hours during the winter. It was something I would have to get used to being away from.

My phone rang and I picked it up instantly. "Hello?" I said. "What's up, motherfucker," Star's voice echoed. I hadn't talked to him in some time. He was already on the outside and studying for some community college exams. They were going to take place a few days after that call. He had gotten parole about a year before I did. I got some tips from him. His tone sounded so much more positive, compared to when we were in the desert together. He was a new man.

"How are you feeling?" he asked.

"I'm nervous, man," I responded.

"I know you are, bro. Just wear everything on your sleeve. Show 'em what you are now," he said.

"What I am is a convicted killer. There's no way..."

"Can you hold on a beat, Dave? I'll be right back." Star said.

Before I could answer, the call was muted. I could hear nothing on the other end. I started to think. The board would be half its size today and comprised two members, the Commissioner, and the Deputy Commissioner. The mothers of my victims would also be present. It was not something I was looking forward to, but it was a necessity in my life. I had to keep trying, for my mom. She would not have died in vain. Neither would Will or Auntie Cheryl. I wanted to be David Spivey again.

"You still there, Dave?" Star's voice suddenly echoed.

"Yeah," I responded.

"I got a surprise for you... Make yourself known for Dave," Star said with high energy.

There was a brief moment of silence. I wasn't sure what was happening, and as I opened my mouth to speak, a familiar voice bellowed through the speaker. "What's up, asshole!" Eric's voice boomed. I couldn't believe it. Star and Eric didn't know each other. I was the mutual, the bridge, the connection, and there we were, on a conference call.

"Star was sayin' you're nervous, man. That's the point. If you're nervous about something it means you care," Eric said. He was right and I knew it. I cared a lot. I was so invested that the thought of failure could have caused a rupture inside me and crumbled me from within. "You're gonna' do great, man. Next time you speak to us you're gonna have your release date, and the time after that you're gonna be in a

Halfway House, and then after that, it's nothing but total freedom," Star said.

"Make me jealous, bro. Good luck,' Eric added.

The pitter-patter sound of my footsteps tapping against the grated metal walkways filled the air. I strolled alongside Officer Bailey. We were silent. The eyes of inmates in their cells followed me as I walked by them. I could sense their desperation. I could feel the hot air blowing through the bars and at my feet. It didn't matter anymore. I was immune to the hate. Ahead of us was Earl. He stood by a set of double doors, spinning his keys around his index finger.

"Look what we have here!" he yelled out.

Earl shook my hand with a tight grasp and looked into my eyes. "Remember what we talked about. Will and intention," he said. Earl was a guiding light in my life. He showed me a future that I wasn't sure I could have. He was a natural-born teacher and he used his own experience to get through to me. I knew I would be forever grateful for his help. "Thank you," I mumbled. He slammed his hand down on my shoulder with great pressure. It was a fatherly kind of expression of love.

"Good luck, David," Officer Bailey spoke, before stepping away.

I stood nervously outside of the boardroom. Earl was by my side and a young guard leaned against the wall and watched my every breath. It was always the immature ones that had a warped view of inmates and prisons. Sure, most of us were con men who manipulated people the first chance we got. But, not all of us were. Some of us genuinely wanted to improve. That understanding would come through experience alone.

"Stop looking at the guard, Dave. Focus on the room," Earl said to me.

The door opened and an old black woman stood in the doorway. She wore pearls around her neck and a black dress. Beyond her was a long brown table, where a man sat alongside the mothers of my victims. "Come on in, David," she said. I entered the space to find a slight chill in the air. All eight eyes were gazing at me. I sat in a plastic chair opposite the four of them. I interlocked my fingers and put my hands on the icy table.

"Mr. Spivey, my name is Janice and this is Gene. I'm the Commissioner, and Gene is the Deputy Commissioner. I'm sure you are familiar with the women to my left. Today is your second parole hearing and we will be discussing the crimes you committed, your gang affiliations, and your psychology. Do you have any questions before we begin?" Janice exclaimed.

"No Ma'am," I responded.

Janice was like a vicious hound who barked an inch from your face but would not bite. Gene was more quiet, but his questions hit hard. I was asked about specific details of the murder. They wanted to know what was going through my mind when I pulled the trigger not only once, but multiple times. "Murder was on my mind. I was determined to prove to my gang that I was capable of doing whatever it would take to rule the neighborhood. It ultimately all came down to me, and it was my doing. I regret my decision every single day," I told them.

The truth was imperative to success. These people heard lies every single day. They could sniff them out, and I was not a smart enough man to fool them. "Mr. Spivey, I'm concerned about your gang affiliations. Who's to say that you don't slip back into crime the second you're released?" Gene asked.

"I can assure you that those days are behind me. I still love my brothers, because they are the ones who are there for me when I need them, but I refuse to condone their actions any longer. I have stepped away completely. I don't even stand with the boys in the yard anymore. If you know anything about prison, you'd know how dangerous it is to be alone," I responded.

They knew that was the truth. The file they had for me was huge, but most of it was from my time on the streets and in juvie. There was nothing they could pin against me from when I was incarcerated. "Now that you bring up the gang's activity in prison, I'm curious about your time in the Gym. There was a significant fatality the day your mother died, no?" Janice inquired. Officer Jacob had mentioned my name in his report of the events that night.

"Blood was spilled near my feet but I had no involvement. My shoes stayed dry. As for the rest of my time in the Gym, I was quiet. I had my head on a swivel and I would be lying if I told you that I was not ready for a fight at any moment, because I truly was. But, I promise to you that I never tarnished a single soul but my own while I was within those walls. I had positive influences to thank for that," I responded.

The mothers held their heads low a lot of the time. I knew how difficult it was for them to even look at me. I was the man who murdered one of their children and attempted to murder the other. I was the devil, a dog that needed to be put down. My arms shook but I took a deep breath through my nostrils to remain steady. Janice and Gene organized the loose files in their hands and both of them cleared the phlegm from their throats at the exact same time.

"I have a question for you, Mr. Spivey, and I want you to take a moment to think about your answer," Janice said.

"Yes ma'am," I responded.

"You are a convicted murderer. You joined a gang when you were barely a teenager. You've beaten people up for no reason, stolen goods for your own benefit, and sold drugs to supplement a street lifestyle. You did all of this before you even became a man. You have never been an adult in society. You have only matured in the confines of a cell. So, tell me... Why do you think that you should be eligible for parole?" Janice asked.

Two shots and my life was over. I was seventeen years old and I was filled with angst. I deserved everything that came to me. If I had gotten away with it, who knows how many I would have killed and how many lives I would have ruined. My presence was toxic. Straight up, I was a danger to society. I was everything the previous parole board had told me I was. However, I knew deep within me that I had changed. I never wanted to do anybody wrong ever again. I knew that much to be true.

"I am deeply sorry for what I did. I was raised by a loving mother and it was my choice to ignore that love and seek validation from the vicious men that ruled my neighborhood. My mother knew the path that I was on and she tried to stop me but I was a runaway train. Prison is what slammed the breaks. I deserve to be here, not just for what I did, but for what I was going to do if I had not been caught. During my time in incarceration, I've had a whole lot of nightmares. I've been chased through dark prisons by a shadowy silhouette with red eyes since my first night in a cell. I've seen the corpses of my mother and brother in terrifying flashes of light while I slept. My mind is consumed by the consequences of the choices I have made. I deserve this. But, the other night I had a dream. It was my first dream in incarceration that didn't cause me to jolt awake in the middle of the night, covered in sweat. It made me feel warm and hopeful, and it is this dream that will inspire me to continue living, even for a short while... I will have to watch the murder of your son and the attempted murder of yours on repeat for eternity. I know I deserve everything that has happened to me and everything that will happen to me. So, to answer your question, I can sit here and try to convince you that I'm eligible for parole, but in the end, it is the board's decision and my answer can only reflect how I feel inside. I want you to see my desire for release, and the intentions of my actions to get myself there."

I just wanted to prove to my mom that I was capable of great things even though it would take a lifetime of convincing. I was ready for whatever answer they had for me. At that point, it did not matter. I had said what I needed to say. Anything more would have been overkill. I was sorry, and I needed them to know I felt remorse for my actions, and that I was not just remorseful for getting caught. Earl had proved to me that will and intention were king, not excuses. I did what I did and my actions had to show that I was moving on. The meeting was coming to an end, and I awaited those fateful words.

"Mr. Spivey, you have spent fifteen years incarcerated and the board recognizes the toll that takes on someone's body. We appreciate your honesty and attention to detail when it comes to answering our questions. The board also recognizes your attempts to self-improve. From your non-profit, to physically separating yourself from your gang, we do see the intent. However, you are still a murderer. That is a title you are going to have to carry around for the rest of your life. That is something that most men cannot handle. They get released and one day some guy crosses them on the street and they revert back to the mindset they had in prison and they beat them to death. It happens all the time, and that's why there are so many repeat offenders... For us to let you go, we have to decide for ourselves if that is something that could happen to you. I think it could, but I also think it could happen to anyone. We are all human. You just happen to be someone with a record, and because of that, there is less trust. At your worst, you kill people. At my worst, I get a parking ticket. You are right. You do deserve to be here... But, Mr. Spivey, I admire your motivation, especially in the time that has passed since your first parole hearing. Your growth is apparent and the truth in your words is convincing. I, and the board, believe you are eligible for parole."

My world stopped spinning and everything became still. A wave of feelings rushed through me. The love in my blood slithered to my heart and I could feel the organ thumping against the inside of my chest. I trembled in the plastic chair with every inhale. The tips of my fingers were perspiring and I tapped them against my thigh. I simply did not know what to say. The words were held captive in my throat by my emotions. I had been waiting years to hear those words.

"Thank you," I managed to let out.

The torment inside me had fallen to a lull. The clouds parted and the light of my life shone through. I felt a warmth within me for the first time in my adult life. I had to wait 120 days for my release, and when that was over, I said goodbye to my cell for the last time. I looked inside it and I said to myself that I would never see the sight of it or anything like it again. That part of my life was over. I walked through the institution and gazed around at the place I had called home. Good riddance. The guards all watched as I left and a few of them even waved to me. I was given some belongings and told that a friend was outside to pick me up. I didn't know who. I had thought that all of my friends had left me in the past. I had come to terms with that before I even became incarcerated.

The doors of the prison were opened for me by Officer Bailey. We exchanged no words as I stepped into the light and had the door slammed behind me. The noise echoed across the plains and all the way to the street, where an old, gray Toyota was parked. Dust blew along the ground. The air rushed over my skin. The door of the vehicle opened. My eyes grew wide and a smile struck my face.

"You didn't think I'd let you take a cab home, did you, motherfucker?" Star said.

I rushed toward him. He came at me. We embraced each other as free men. The blistering hot sun beat down on us but we were wearing our own clothes and we had our own lives to go ahead and live. The horizon was vast and far away but I told Star to kick it and drive right for it. My time in incarceration was over, and it was my intention to make up for the crimes I had committed by being a voice for young men who were at risk of following my tumultuous past. That ember glow of the falling sun will forever be imprinted in my mind. I knew my loved ones were watching me through its glowing lens, and I would not disappoint them again. Before I was a criminal, I was a kid who played video games with his friends and screwed around in class. I am a convicted killer and a reformed gang member. These are all labels that will forever be attached to my name. Yet, I know who I am. I am David Spivey.

THE END.

Dedications

"To my beautiful mother Linda M. Bailey, may you rest in peace. I hope I've made you proud. Willy Will, my dear brother, I miss and love you so much. Rest well until we meet again. Thanks to my Aunt Terri L. Bailey, who made my dream of being home became a reality. I never had to worry because she always reminded me that things would be okay. Margaret Beemon, my Granny Gran, you're my number one lady, and I love you so much. Aunt Alice M. Goll, when I felt trapped, you showed me love and reassured me that it was just a part of my journey. Your love and support meant everything. Thanks to my family - Darrell, Aunt Adlean, Marlo Mooney Martin, and Myla - for always believing in me and remembering who I am, not just what I've done."

— David Spivey

Questions you might be asking yourself

How did an Irish author meet a former LA gang member?
Cillian met David on New Years Eve, 2022. David was a security guard, and Cillian was the bar manager. Not too many people showed up to the event, so Cillian and David had the chance to chat for a few hours, even though David was more interested in talking to the cute budtender that was selling joints at a booth by the security stand. It was on this night that the two developed a friendship, and several months later, Cillian officially started to interview David with the intention of writing this very book.

What is David doing now?
As of the release of this book, David is a successful motivational speaker and mental health professional. His social media presence is constantly growing and his 'anti-crime' and 'anti-gang life' message is helping young people change their lives. He hopes to one day have this book adapted into a film.

Just how true is this story?
Everything that happens in the book, happened in reality. Cillian did take the liberty of exaggerating certain aspects of the plot to increase digestibility for the audience, but for the most part, the inmates and their actions are accurate to the truth. Additionally, David and Cillian spent one month together so that Cillian could interview him and be aided in developing the story to ensure that the characters, plot, and themes are all accurate to David's experience.

What is the purpose of the dream sequences in the book?

While interviewing David, Cillian noticed that a lot of the stories that were being told revolved around the mind. It became clear to the author that inmates spend most of their time in incarceration fighting battles in their head. David was no different, and the dreams that are outlined in the book are dreams that David actually experienced during his time in incarceration.

STAY UPDATED

Follow the socials below to stay updated on Dave's progress as a motivational speaker.

Dave's Instagram
@realrecognizereal_podcast

Book updates
@dreams_in_incarceration

DON'T FORGET TO REVIEW THE BOOK ON GOODREADS!
Every review helps.

Thank you for reading.

Cillian & Dave.

Printed in Great Britain
by Amazon